"What Is It That You Want, Rachel?"

John asked. "Do you want me to make love to you again, so you can prove just how far I'll go before you leave me? How many times do I have to play the fool?"

"It isn't that at all," she said miserably. But she shivered as she thought of the pleasure his lovemaking had brought her.

"The hell it isn't," he ground out. "If you came back here to prove something, I'm not going to be any part of it. Why don't you go play games with your son's father?"

Rachel nearly said the words, the pronouncement that would stop John cold. But she couldn't. Not when he was in such anguish. Not when the truth would cause him even more pain.

"I told you," she said huskily. "David's father doesn't see us anymore."

Dear Reader,

As always, I am proud to be bringing you the very best that romance has to offer—starting with an absolutely wonderful *Man of the Month* from Annette Broadrick called *Mysterious Mountain Man*. A book from Annette is always a real treat, and I know this story—her fortieth for Silhouette—will satisfy her fans and gain her new ones!

As readers, you've told me that you *love* miniseries, and you'll find some of the best series right here at Silhouette Desire. This month we have *The Cop and the Chorus Girl*, the second book in Nancy Martin's delightful *Opposites Attract* series, and *Dream Wedding*, the next book in Pamela Macaluso's *Just Married* series.

For those who like a touch of the supernatural, look for Linda Turner's *Heaven Can't Wait*. Lass Small's many fans will be excited about her latest, *Impulse*. And Kelly Jamison brings us a tender tale about a woman who returns to her hometown to confront her child's father in *Forsaken Father*.

Don't miss any of these great love stories!

Lucia Macro,
Senior Editor

Please address questions and book requests to:
Silhouette Reader Service
U.S.: 3010 Walden Ave., P.O. Box 1325, Buffalo, NY 14269
Canadian: P.O. Box 609, Fort Erie, Ont. L2A 5X3

KELLY
JAMISON
FORSAKEN FATHER

SILHOUETTE *Desire*™

Published by Silhouette Books

America's Publisher of Contemporary Romance

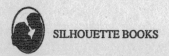

SILHOUETTE BOOKS

ISBN 0-373-05930-2

FORSAKEN FATHER

Copyright © 1995 by Linda Buechting

Printed in U.S.A.

Books by Kelly Jamison

Silhouette Desire

Echoes from the Heart #579
Hearts in Hiding #626
Heartless #760
Will #798
The Daddy Factor #885
*Forsaken Father #930

*McClennon Family

KELLY JAMISON

grew up in a small town and often makes rural communities the settings for her books. After her college graduation, she worked for a newspaper that was so tiny it didn't even have its own camera. Whenever a staff member needed to take a picture, she'd borrow a camera from the woman next door.

Kelly is a rabid chocoholic and pizza addict who also paints in watercolors and rides her bike. She has also written as Kelly Adams.

One

Rachel Tucker paused on the threshold of the Nu View Restaurant, overcome with homesickness even though she was finally home. It was a homesickness born of suppressed memories and the need to let her old life catch up with her before she went through the door.

It had hit her in a rush when she got off the small commuter plane in the airport, which sat practically in the middle of a cornfield. This was Pierce, Illinois, named after a hardy pioneer who came up the Mississippi River in the 1800s, took one look at the fertile floodplain and decided that this was the place he and his descendants would call home.

This was where Rachel Tucker had grown into a woman.

She was coming home to stay this time, and she was bringing John David McClennon's son with her.

Shading her eyes and peering through the glass, she saw a scattering of customers lingering over coffee and gossip. Rachel shivered slightly in the chill air. It had rained on and off for most of the months of April and May in Pierce and

surrounding Carson County. This much rain was unprece-
dented in early June, and no one in Pierce knew quite what
to expect. In fact, it had rained all up and down the Mississippi River, and that was what had brought her back to
Pierce.

The Mississippi was threatening to top record heights,
scaling the tallest levees and destroying valuable farmland.
Rachel owned a small piece of that farmland, and though
hers sat safely on a bluff, she felt drawn home to help others in any way she could. She had grown up with these people, had attended their weddings and funerals, had drawn
comfort from them when her parents died.

The only person, other than her brother, who knew she
was coming was George Edwards, the local bank owner and
old family friend. She was meeting him here.

The bell tinkled when she pushed open the door, and all
the customers looked up, eager for a fresh voice to join the
afternoon discourse on crops, weather and life in general.
She moved toward a booth in the back, scanning faces,
when a familiar voice called out teasingly, "Rachel Tucker,
is that really you?"

Rachel turned with a ready smile. "George, how are
you?"

Her smile faltered when she saw who was sitting in the
booth next to George. Her eyes skittered away and across
the table to George's wife, Rowena. She managed to nod
and return Rowena's greeting before she looked back at
John David McClennon's piercing stare. He hadn't spoken, which didn't surprise her in the least. What did surprise her was to see him sitting here with George. He must
have had no idea she was coming.

"Hello, John," she said, hoping she sounded normal. It
was an effort to continue looking into his deep blue eyes
without flinching. She knew what he thought of her. And if
she hadn't known before, the hard look on his face confirmed it now. He believed she had left him for another man
eleven years ago.

And she had let him believe it.

"Rachel," he acknowledged, his voice a rasp that was as harsh as his eyes. Both men had risen slightly, and she gestured them back into their seats.

"Maybe this isn't a good time," she said hesitantly to George. It had caught her off guard, seeing John so unexpectedly, and she didn't know how to handle the situation.

"Nonsense, honey," he insisted as Rowena scooted over to make room for Rachel. "Sit yourself down, and let's catch up. I was just telling John that you're here to check on your property."

Rachel nodded as she settled herself, trying not to look at John. His hair was as black as she remembered, but now with some gray at the sides. He would be thirty-three, she thought. He still exuded the same power and sheer will. He was dressed in jeans, dirty, as though he'd been working in the rain, and a black sweatshirt with the sleeves cut off. He sat with his arms crossed over his chest, looking relaxed as he leaned back in the booth. But Rachel knew that he was anything but relaxed at the moment. She wondered briefly if he hated her for what she'd done.

"I'm here for another reason as well," Rachel said, deciding to be direct. "I'm worried about Mason. He called me about a week ago, and he didn't sound at all good." Mason wouldn't give her any specifics on the phone, but Rachel had heard unspoken anxiety in her brother's voice.

"He's had some problems, but he's doing all right," John said cautiously.

"What kind of problems?" Rachel demanded, meeting his gaze and nearly flinching at the coldness there.

"Nothing that concerns you."

"Mason's my brother, and it does concern me," she snapped, refusing to tolerate his condescending attitude.

John glared at her. "He's gotten along so far without your help."

He wasn't talking about Mason anymore, and they both knew it.

So this was how it would be, Rachel thought in resignation. She had come back home to live under the judgment of John's anger. She guessed she was a fool to have supposed he would be civil to her given the fact that he had married shortly after she left. Rachel had thought Meredith Thompson an unlikely wife for John, but it was his choice to make.

George cleared his throat uncomfortably, apparently acutely aware that he was in the middle of an undercurrent he hadn't foreseen. "Well, I'm sure things will work out," he said. "And he'll be glad to see Rachel." He glanced from Rachel to John, then cleared his throat again.

"Where are you staying, dear?" Rowena asked Rachel, giving her husband a look that said, *You definitely need some help here.*

"That's what I wanted to talk to you about," Rachel said, but before she could say any more, the waitress arrived for their orders.

Rachel and John wanted only coffee, but George and Rowena, stalwart food enthusiasts, ordered cheeseburgers and fries. John caught Rachel looking at him while he ordered, and his eyes held hers challengingly.

He hadn't thought she'd still be as pretty as he remembered, but she was. Her blond hair was shorter than she'd worn it eleven years ago, but he liked the way it turned under at her chin. Hell, he thought, he couldn't afford to like anything about Rachel Tucker. Not after the way she'd ended their relationship. He'd thought he would feel a suffocating anger when he saw her, but instead he felt an ache deep inside. He forced himself to continue looking at her, and finally her green eyes wavered and lowered to the table.

When the waitress left, Rachel made herself look at George and pretend that John wasn't there, an almost impossible task given his commanding presence.

"I was thinking of staying in Dad's old summer cabin, the one he left you," she said. "Besides adjoining my land, it overlooks the river. I've always liked that place, and it's high on the bluff and safe from the flood. That is, if you don't mind, George."

George rubbed the back of his neck absently. "I don't know, Rachel. It's awfully lonely up there. And nobody's stayed there in years."

"I'm willing to pay for repairs. And whatever rent you'd like. I just don't want you to feel pressured if you're still using it. I know you've gone there now and then since Dad died."

She looked like an eager child, John thought. So many years ago he'd found that face captivating. When Rachel was enthralled with something, it was written all over her face, giving her a vibrancy that would steal your breath away. A long time ago she was enthralled with him.

"I haven't used it at all in a couple of years," George said slowly. "These old bones don't get around like they used to. But John's been keeping an eye on the place for me. I don't know what kind of shape it's in, but I can't think of any reason why you can't stay there if you want."

"I know a reason," John interjected. "We're all working long hours right now sandbagging the levees. I don't know when I can get to those repairs."

"I don't expect you to do the repairs," Rachel said brusquely. "And until I can get someone to do them, I'll take the cabin in its current condition."

John snorted derisively. "The cabin isn't an apartment in Boston, Rachel. It's in worse shape than you think."

"I don't care." She stuck her chin out at him. "I want to stay there. I'll pay whatever the repairs cost."

"I'm sure money is no object," John said, and she heard the derision in his tone again. "A person can buy almost anything, can't they, Rachel?"

She understood what he left unspoken, but she ignored it. She was tired, and she was feeling lousy because of a cold, but she wasn't going to let John McClennon ruin her homecoming.

"What about it, George?" she asked quietly, training her gaze on him.

"Oh, for heaven's sake, George," Rowena interrupted. "Let the girl stay there. Rachel knows how to take care of herself. And John can do some repair work when he has time."

Rachel smiled her thanks at Rowena. In their seventies now, George and Rowena had been like surrogate grandparents to her when she was growing up. It was George who had steered her into banking, George who had given her her first summer job and then written a glowing letter of recommendation to the state college.

"All right then," George said, slapping the table with his palm. "I guess the cabin is yours." He fished in his pocket and brought out a key ring laden with a dozen keys of various shapes and sizes. "Let's see here." He fumbled with each key, mumbling its purpose as he went around the ring. "House—front door, house—back door, garage, office—front door, office—"

"What are you, George, a banker or a locksmith?" John complained. "You carry enough keys to open every house in town."

"A good banker comes prepared, right, Rachel?" He winked at Rachel, and she smiled back.

"Thank you, George," she said as he pulled off the right key and slid it across the table to her.

Their coffee and cheeseburgers came, but John elbowed George. "I have to leave," he said shortly, throwing a dollar bill onto the table and impatiently leaning over George.

"Hey, what's the rush?" George asked good-naturedly, sliding out of the booth so John could get past.

"I've got things to do," John rumbled.

Rachel had almost forgotten how tall he was. When he straightened to his full height, she had to look up at a sharp angle to see his face. Six feet, four inches, if she remembered correctly. He was still glaring at her, but she was determined not to let him intimidate her. She was here, and it was going to be on her own terms, not his.

"Say hello to Meredith," she said politely.

"Yeah, sure," he replied sarcastically, turning on his heel and slamming out the door before she could say anything else.

George and Rowena were both studying grease stains on the table when Rachel turned around. "Well?" she demanded.

"He's been divorced from Meredith for almost five years now, honey," Rowena informed her.

"Oh. I didn't know." Rachel leaned back and looked out the door, seeing a blue pickup truck with John at the wheel leaving the parking lot in a trail of spewing gravel. He was not a happy man, and she knew she had a lot to do with that.

She'd had no idea he was divorced. She had purposely avoided keeping in touch with anyone from Pierce. She didn't want to know if John McClennon was happy or miserable or so angry that he could look at her with loathing in his eyes, the way he had looked at her today.

George and Rowena exchanged looks again, something that didn't escape Rachel's notice.

"Have you seen your brother yet?" George asked.

Rachel shook her head. "I thought I'd stop by Mason's place on my way to the cabin. Is he still at the same apartment?"

This time the exchanged looks were unmistakable.

"Yes, he is, but, honey, don't you keep up with him at all?" Rowena asked.

"Of course," Rachel said. "I guess I forgot his address." It wasn't true. Mason had remained aloof and silent when she left town, and she rarely heard from him until the week before. There was cause for alarm when Mason made a phone call, and this one had worried her enough that she rushed her plans to return to town.

"The same place on Front Street," George said. He reached over and patted her hand. "Rachel, are you okay?"

"I'm fine," she assured him. "I've been fighting a cold for a few days. I'm just a little run-down." She swallowed the last of her coffee and stood. "I'd better head up to the cabin and check it out. I really appreciate your letting me rent it."

"It's no problem, honey," George said, his brow furrowed.

"Rachel," Rowena said, catching Rachel's hand when she would have moved to the door. "How is your boy?"

"David's fine," Rachel said, her voice softening. "He's flying here in two days when his soccer camp is over."

"How old is he now?" Rowena asked. She and George had no children, but she always discussed the subject with the enthusiasm of a grandmother. No one but Mason knew that David was John's child, and Rachel had sworn Mason to silence.

"He'll be eleven next birthday."

"You stop and see Mason," Rowena advised her. "He'll want to hear all about what his nephew's doing."

Rachel nodded and moved to the door. *Oh, Lord,* she thought as she went out into the gathering wind. *This was going to be harder than she'd thought.*

When she pulled up to Mason's apartment in the rental car, her brother was just going to his own car. Rachel parked and caught up with him before he pulled away. Front Street was on the river, and the apartments were mostly over taverns and small used-furniture shops. The river was out of its banks here, and sandbags lined the fronts of the sidewalks. Rachel could see the flagpoles of the riverfront park jutting out of the water. That meant the picnic area and fountain were all flooded.

"What are you doing here?" Mason said in surprise as Rachel leaned in the driver's window and ruffled his hair. Her smile faded when she saw the lines around his eyes and the pallor of his skin.

"I'm home to check on the property." The land Rachel's father had left her adjoined the land with the cabin he'd left to George. "I'm going to stay in Dad's old summer cabin." Rachel paused. "Mason, what's been happening with you?"

"Nothing."

"There has to be something," Rachel persisted. "You didn't sound like yourself on the phone."

"Listen, I've got to be somewhere now," Mason said, putting the car into drive. "I'll catch you later."

Rachel backed away and sighed as her brother pulled from the curb. That was Mason, always on his way somewhere. But he never quite got there. He reminded her of the prince in countless fairy tales, his life soured by an evil witch. Mason was charming, kind and sensitive. Maybe too sensitive. At any rate, he seemed perpetually cursed with bad luck. His lovers left him, and he lost one job after another. His latest career move was to buy a tavern on this street. Rachel wondered if his phone call had been prompted by some setback there.

Rachel went to her own car and sat behind the wheel, feeling more tired than she had in her whole life. She had thought that coming back here would be so simple. She had thought that it was the kind of community David needed. And if she were honest with herself, she had thought that she could see John McClennon and not feel this stomach-churning anxiety.

She was afraid she'd made a mistake coming back. She would never survive John's cold indifference. She remembered when things between them were far different, and she ached for those days.

She and John had grown up together, fast friends despite the three-year difference in their ages. John was never anything but patient and kind to her. It was no wonder she fell in love with him.

Remarkably, to her, he loved her, too. She was the product of a broken marriage. Her father, dead fifteen years now, had been absent most of her life. Her mother was...

Her mother was the kind of woman who would sleep with the next man who came along whether he wore a wedding ring or not. Rachel had learned early to stand defiantly silent when the children at school taunted her. But John David McClennon always stood up for her.

John and his brothers had faced their own share of teasing. The farm and house were all the family had, and making ends meet in lean years was an impossible challenge.

John often showed up at school with his older brother, Jake's, hand-me-down clothes. His mother patched them, but it was difficult to hide how worn they were.

John withstood the teasing with quiet stoicism and an easy grace that won him a lot of friends. He was a superb athlete, and soon that and his scholastic abilities eclipsed any deficiency in his clothing.

John's father died when he was in college, and he and Rachel drew closer together, as though gathering a ring of protection around themselves.

It was when she went away to school herself three years later that things began to change. She realized that she didn't want to stay in Pierce. She wanted to escape the taunts she still remembered, escape the small town for a big city.

John didn't understand. He was a big football hero in college, an honor student whose fame spread far and wide, but still he wanted nothing more than the house and farm in Pierce. He reminded Rachel of the many people who had been kind to her during childhood and beyond, but still she wanted to be someplace else. If only she could have John with her.

John came home from college and began building a life in Pierce, while Rachel finished college.

The night that Rachel graduated with a job offer from an investment firm in San Francisco, she and John made love, then got into the worst argument of their long relationship. There was a chasm of difference between what each wanted in life.

She left town the next day, expecting John to call her despite the fact that she had left every present he ever gave her on his doorstep that morning. But she didn't hear from him.

It was the night she moved into her new apartment that Rachel discovered she was pregnant. She didn't know how to tell John. She knew him well enough to know that he would do the right thing and marry her. And one of them would end up miserable, either in San Francisco or Pierce.

Pride and uncertainty made her put off telling John for a while. Eventually she realized that she wouldn't ever tell him. She knew that he would do the honorable thing and come live with her if that's what she wanted, but she couldn't ask him to do that. She would never trap any man, much less John David McClennon, into coming to her.

It was at an investment conference in Chicago that Rachel ran into a former classmate from high school, who was now a banker in nearby Chicago Heights. Rachel was a month away from delivery, and the woman eyed her expanding waistline speculatively. Rachel knew that within days all of Pierce would know that she was pregnant. Mrs. Tucker's little girl, pregnant and unmarried. Living up to her mother's legacy.

The classmate filled her in on all the news from home, including the fact that John David McClennon was now married. Rachel hadn't thought that it would hurt after all these months, but the news hit like a physical blow.

There was nothing to do but go back to San Francisco and wait for the phone call, the one that would come when John found out that she was pregnant.

He called two weeks later.

Rachel had already formulated and rehearsed her lie. She had met someone, she told him, someone who could give her the things she couldn't find in Pierce.

"His family is . . . well-to-do," she hedged.

"That never mattered to you before," John said, and she heard the pain in his voice. "Or did it?"

"I'm tired of making do," she said. "I want more." It was hurting her to say what she had to say, to know what she was doing to John, but it had to be done harshly. Otherwise, John would press her until he found out that the baby was his, and then he would ruin his life trying to make it right for her.

"Does he like big cities?"

"Yes."

"But how could you have met him so soon?" John insisted. "I heard that your baby is about due. Unless—" He broke off, and Rachel heard the catch in his voice. "Unless you were seeing him the same time you were with me."

Rachel didn't say anything, knowing that he would draw his own conclusions from her silence.

"You were seeing another man and didn't have the decency to *tell* me!" he accused. "Hell, Rachel, you sure had me fooled. That's what you did, isn't it? Played me for the fool."

Rachel knew from his voice that she'd done what she set out to do. John McClennon would never want to see her again. She had wounded him where no one else ever had.

"And what about Meredith?" Rachel asked quietly. "Why didn't you tell me about her?"

"Because there was nothing to tell until well after you left me," he said bitterly.

In the background a woman called from another room. Meredith. Rachel felt her throat closing in pain. She would always love John David McClennon, whether he loved her or not, but she would not use his baby to make him leave his wife. Her mother had ruined more than one marriage in her time, but Rachel had vowed never to stoop to that level.

"I'm glad you're gone from here, Rachel," John said bitterly. "Because if I ever see you again, I won't be responsible for what I do."

He slammed down the receiver, making Rachel jump.

It was the right thing to do, Rachel told herself over and over. With the shortsightedness of youth, she believed it was the *only* thing to do.

But being right was cold comfort in an empty bed. And the beds seemed to get colder and emptier as she was transferred from one city to another, finally ending up in Boston.

She carried her one suitcase into the cabin, having to really lean on the door to get it open after she unlocked it. It was a good-size cabin with a bedroom and an open, inviting kitchen with a breakfast bar that led into the living room. A small bathroom was off the bedroom.

She had sometimes spent summer nights here with George and Rowena, lying in her sleeping bag on the couch and gazing dreamily as shadows from the trees outside the window danced on the fireplace. It was almost a magical place to her, the place where she had first realized she really could make something more of herself than her mother had. It was the place where she and John had played. It overlooked John's farm and land, the house that belonged to his parents when she was a child. She had always felt safe here.

She brushed a cobweb from the corner of the stone fireplace, thinking of those shadows from long ago.

"I told you it needs a lot of work."

She jumped when she heard his voice behind her. He must have walked from his house; she hadn't heard his truck. He was standing in the doorway, blocking the light, his powerful body thrown into deep shadow with the sun behind him.

"It's livable," she said, trying to control her breathing.

He made a noise of disgust and walked into the room. She silently trailed on his heels as he made his inspection. He opened the closet door in the kitchen and checked the hot-water heater before turning it on. He kept looking at the ceiling and shaking his head. Rachel followed his gaze and saw brown spots and loose plaster. Leaks, she supposed. He plugged in the refrigerator, frowning over the coils.

He went on to the bathroom and turned on the water to the toilet, then checked the shower. "Shower head's rusty," he told her. "You'll have to take it off and soak it."

Rachel nodded. Nothing insurmountable so far. He still hadn't looked at her.

The bedroom was last. One look around, and he said, "You can't sleep here."

"Why not?" she demanded.

He pointed at the ceiling, then the floor. "Look at that. The floorboards are rotting from water standing on them. And a big chunk of plaster could fall any time."

"I'll put a bucket under the leak."

"That won't solve anything."

"Then I'll sleep on the couch in the other room." She was tired of his objections. He could give her as many reasons as he wanted, but she was staying.

She started when he stepped closer, his eyes darkening in fierceness.

"Why are you doing this, Rachel?" he demanded. "What's so damn important that it brought you all the way back here?"

She stared back at him, but wouldn't answer. She couldn't tell him if she wanted. She knew all the reasons she'd given herself, the increasing peer pressures on a child like David in a big school, the rising crime rate in a large city, dissatisfaction with her job, the urgency of checking out her property in the face of the Midwest's flooding. But she sensed that none of these was the real reason that had brought her back.

As if he, too, sensed that there was more here than he wanted to know, John abruptly stepped back, his eyes still smoldering.

He spun on his heel, and she followed him to the living room. He was kneeling, inspecting the fireplace, when he looked up at her. "This is where you kept that baby crow while you nursed him back to health."

She stared at him blankly for a moment, having forgotten. Then she remembered, and she almost smiled. She had rescued that crow from a neighbor's cat and taken it to a vet. With its wing set, she brought it home and gave it residence right in front of the fireplace. Soon the crow thought he owned the entire living room, and he would eat cornflakes from Rachel's hand. She and John had solemnly taken him outside when he could fly again and turned him loose. He hung around the yard for days, begging for a handout, then finally left.

Rachel had cried, and John had held her. Remembering now, she felt a sharp ache.

John abruptly stood. "How could you care so much about a crow and nothing for me and your life here?"

Before she could say anything, he clamped his hands on her shoulders, his strong fingers digging into them. The touch was like electricity to her nerve endings. She felt a shiver run through the core of her being.

"Did you grow to hate me so much, Rachel, that you could take up with another man while you were making love to me?"

"I never hated you," she whispered hoarsely, shaking her head.

He was silent a long, tense moment, the only sound his harsh breathing. "Tell me one thing. Did he make you happy when I couldn't?" he demanded, abruptly releasing her.

She stepped back, her eyes wide.

She should tell him the truth now, she told herself. But she didn't want John to find out about his son in a moment of anger.

"Yes," she said evenly, "he did."

John's eyes darkened. "Are you married to him?"

Rachel shook her head.

John's eyes pinned her for a long moment while she held her breath.

"I'll be back with Mom in the morning to clean the house," he said, his voice under control again.

He turned and walked out the door, leaving her to stare after him, the imprints of his fingers on her flesh bringing back a flood of memories, all of them bittersweet.

Two

Rachel was too restless to stay in the cabin after John left. The memory of his cold glare and the touch of his hands on her shoulders made her tremble.

She drove to the grocery store to put him out of her mind.

She was putting grocery bags in her rental car when a young man hailed her from across the lot.

"Rachel! I heard you were back in town!" He jogged to her and stuck out his hand. "You probably don't remember me. I'm John's brother Jordan."

"Oh, Jordan! Of course." Rachel took his hand and shook it. "I didn't know you lived here."

"I don't." He grinned. "I live in St. Louis now. I've got my own electronics company. I took some time off to come help with the sandbagging." He looked her up and down and grinned again. "Hey, you look great."

"Thank you." Rachel smiled. "So you're a big executive now. Congratulations." Jordan was the ladies' man of the three McClennon brothers. Both John and Jake were one-woman men, but Jordan, the youngest of the lot, preferred his women in quantity.

"Executive or not, nobody I know is impressed," he complained. "Hey, listen. We're cooking at the house tonight. It's becoming kind of a tradition to feed the sandbaggers. Why don't you come by?"

Rachel hesitated. "I haven't done any sandbagging," she reminded him.

"Who cares?" Jordan said. "Come on by anyway. Remember Tiny Harmon? He'll be there."

"It's tempting," she admitted. Tiny was among the friends she valued, though he was old enough to be her father.

"Then we'll see you for dinner. I'll pick you up at seven."

"Wait!" she called as he started to walk away. "Thanks for the ride, Jordan, but I'll walk down."

He was gone the next instant, waving over his shoulder, leaving Rachel to ponder the Pierce grapevine that had already spread the word that she was back. She supposed information had been relayed as to where she was staying, because Jordan hadn't asked.

She was sure that John didn't want to see her again, but she reasoned that there would be a lot of people at his house tonight. She could stay out of his way fairly easily. The McClennon house was huge, and she was well-acquainted with it from childhood.

Driving home, she realized that she knew little about John's family anymore. Jordan was running an electronics company. She grinned again. That suited him. He must have women falling all over him.

She knew that John's older brother, Jake, had been a building contractor, but she had no idea what he was doing now.

And what about John? she wondered as she unloaded groceries in the cabin. What had happened with his marriage? She remembered Meredith Thompson as a pretty brunette who had been on the cheerleading squad. She was two years older than Rachel, which would make her thirty-two now. She knew that John had seen Meredith occasionally while Rachel was away at college, mostly to help her through the loan process for the dress shop she was opening in town. With his head for business, John was always on call for one friend or another.

Rachel felt a pang of what could only be described as jealousy as she thought of John and Meredith alone in the shop, their heads bent together over the books.

It was too late to worry about that now, she assured herself. They were already married and divorced.

She checked her watch and decided to change clothes before dinner.

Rachel walked down the hill just before seven, dressed in khaki pants, a dark blue long-sleeved blouse and sneakers. She'd tied her red cardigan around her neck for warmth.

The summer cabin sat on top of a bluff overlooking the floodplain. The five-hundred-acre McClennon farm was below, sprawling from the river back to the county road. The slope down to the farm was gentle, but Rachel was winded when she got to the bottom from scrambling over large outcroppings of limestone.

City girl, she chided herself. She'd been away too long.

She was about a quarter of a mile inland from the river here, but she could see the long row of sandbags piled on top of the levee.

She heard the noise before she reached the back of the house. Pans rattled in the kitchen, adding to the din of voices and banging doors. The frog song she heard during the walk here had faded.

The house looked much as she remembered, white clapboard with green shutters and a wraparound porch that gave it the settled look of a comfortable matron.

She saw John as soon as she turned the corner. He was trying to light the charcoal in the barbecue, hindered by Jordan and his neighbor Tiny Harmon. John had apparently cleaned up since she'd seen him at the restaurant. Now he wore a light blue, short-sleeved pullover and clean jeans.

"You need more lighter fluid," Tiny insisted, waving the can in the air.

"What he needs are some hickory chips," Jordan argued.

"Will you two get away from me?" John said in exasperation. "Tiny, you're going to blow us all to kingdom come with that can of lighter fluid."

"I didn't know you was one of them *touchy* cooks," Tiny said, wounded.

"I'm not touchy," John groused. "I'm—"

He abruptly broke off when he looked up and saw Rachel.

"What are *you* doing here?" he demanded, making her flush. So much for staying out of his way.

"*I* invited her," Jordan said immediately. "And you'd do well not to ask stupid questions like that."

"Is that Rachel?" Tiny demanded, taking off his camouflage hunting cap and fingering it reverently. "Lord, Rachel, you look better than ever. Don't she, John?"

John didn't answer, and Tiny took his eyes from Rachel long enough to prod John with his elbow.

"What is the matter with you?" John said irritably.

"It's not what's the matter with me that's the problem here," Tiny told him.

"Come on, Tiny," Jordan said, taking him by the elbow. "Let's go check the marinade or whatever."

"But I—" Tiny began, looking from John to Rachel. "Oh," he mumbled lamely. "Yeah, let's go check on the whatever."

"I should go inside, too," Rachel said. "I really came to look up old friends."

"I won't bite," John told her.

"You could have fooled me."

His jaw clenched, and he looked at the smoldering charcoal, throwing on another match. Rachel had the fleeting thought that his eyes were blazing enough to light the charcoal themselves.

"All right," he said with cold reason. "You're only going to be in town for a short while. I can be civil that long, I suppose."

Rachel suppressed an exasperated sigh. It wasn't going to be a short time. She was going to live here, though she hadn't told anyone yet.

"That's considerate of you," she said sarcastically.

"Isn't that what you want?" he demanded, turning those blazing eyes on her again.

She didn't know what she wanted, but it wasn't John's icy stares, no matter how masked they were in civility.

"Well, how's the fire coming?" a strained voice asked, and Rachel turned to see Meredith walking toward them, worry in her eyes and female challenge in the sway of her hips.

"Hello, Meredith," Rachel said politely.

Meredith pointedly ignored her and turned to John. "Do we eat soon? I haven't had anything since you and I ate lunch, and, if you remember, that was only a bologna sandwich."

Rachel knew that the reference to lunch was Meredith's not-so-subtle way of letting her know that she and John were still close. Close enough to eat lunch together, anyway.

"That's all any of the sandbaggers had," John replied, somewhat testily.

So she hadn't eaten alone with him.

Rachel looked up as her brother, Mason, rounded the corner of the porch, a bottle of pop in his hand, and sat on an Adirondack chair. Behind him came John's older brother, Jake.

"Excuse me," Rachel said, "but I haven't talked to Mason yet. Nice to see you, Meredith."

It wasn't all that nice to see Meredith, but there was no harm in a little polite lie. Meredith, for her part, didn't answer. Rachel wondered if Meredith knew what had happened between her and John. Knowing John, he wouldn't have told anyone.

Mason appeared lost in thought, and Rachel stood hesitantly with one foot on a porch step until he looked up. He was thinner than she remembered, his too-long, pale blond hair and watery eyes giving him a wraithlike appearance.

"Hi, again," she said, trying to smile. She hadn't talked to Mason in any meaningful way in several years now, and she was realizing how hard it was to pick up threads of old relationships. At the car he had seemed preoccupied. Now he looked slightly more relaxed.

"Jordan said you were coming for dinner," Mason said. Slowly his weathered face broke into a smile. "Well, come here and give me a hug."

She went, needing a hug badly at the moment. Jake tactfully looked away until they were done. Rachel sat on the bench beside the chair, and Jake stood with one booted foot propped on the end of the bench. He leaned over and shook her hand, welcoming her back.

"So how's the world treating you, Mason?" Rachel asked.

"Not so hot lately," he said, shrugging. "Did you know I bought a tavern?"

"Yes, I'd heard. Congratulations."

"Yeah, well, I lost it. Went bankrupt."

"I'm sorry." Mason's business sense had always been erratic at best. He was in and out of more failed deals than she could count. Each failure was inevitably followed by a bout of hard drinking, which made Rachel all the more surprised to see the pop bottle in his hand.

"Hell, you know me," Mason said. "If it weren't for bad luck, I'd have no luck at all."

Both of them smiled, but there was no humor in it.

"John and I've offered Mason a job," Jake informed Rachel. Like John, he had black hair tinged with gray, but where John's eyes were blue, Jake's eyes were gray.

"Seems I'm going to be a farmhand," Mason said.

"It's an honorable profession," John replied, and Rachel turned her head to see him mounting the steps. "But the job may depend on whether or not the levee holds. There may not be a farm left, this year, anyway."

"I'll sandbag for now," Mason said. "And I want to be like everyone else. No pay. I'm volunteering."

"Good man," John murmured quietly, clapping Mason on the shoulder. He leaned back against the wall on the other side of Mason and rubbed a hand over his eyes.

He must be exhausted, Rachel thought. She'd heard in the grocery store that sandbaggers had been working almost nonstop for several days now. With over fifty miles of levees in this particular drainage district, it was long, hard, tedious labor.

It was odd, she thought. There was something different about Mason. And that soda bottle. This was his usual time for a beer. She watched as he took a long swallow.

"How's my nephew?" Mason asked without looking at her.

"Growing like a weed. He'll be here in a couple of days." She leaned her head back and studied Mason. "Mason, are you all right?" she asked. "You seem . . . different."

"Damn that fire," John muttered. "Come on, Rachel. You can help me with it."

"Meredith is heading this way, just dying to help you with it," she said pointedly. He swung his eyes to the left, his scowl deepening as he saw Meredith very definitely headed his way.

"But I asked *you*," he insisted, stepping around and pulling Rachel from the seat by her arm. His fingers were hard and warm, and she found her pulse quickening at his touch.

He pulled her down the steps and toward the grill. Meredith stood glowering as he passed her without a word.

"John, what has gotten into you?" Rachel demanded as they reached the grill and John began digging at the coals. "I was trying to talk to my brother."

"Your brother doesn't need a probing interview right now," he told her. "He lost his business, and he has things on his mind."

"Mason's lost business ventures before," she said. "And I'm his sister. I'm not going to quiz him. I just need to see if he's all right."

"He's all right," John assured her.

"How would you know?" she returned.

"I'd know better than you since you don't live here any-more," he retorted.

Jordan chose that moment to appear with the bratwurst and hamburgers, and John slammed the plate onto the grill's attached tray.

"Here! Cook these!" he barked at Rachel. A second later he stalked off toward the house. Meredith, who had been hovering just at the edge of Rachel's peripheral vision, hurried after him.

"Cook these?" Rachel repeated angrily. "John David McClennon, I haven't cooked on a grill in at least ten years! I can order out Chinese for you or toss a salad, but I do not grill!"

Her breath was wasted. The door had already slammed behind him, and Mason, Jake and Jordan were surveying her with barely contained amusement.

"This isn't funny," she informed them.

"Oh, no, it definitely isn't," Jordan said, trying to contain a grin. "That's our dinner."

"Here," she said, holding out the spatula toward the three. "You guys can cook these."

The trio immediately dispersed, mumbling excuses and coughing discreetly. Talking to herself under her breath, Rachel slapped hamburgers and bratwurst onto the grill. The John she used to know would have remembered that she hated to cook.

But it was no use pining for the John she used to know. She'd given him no reason to treat her kindly.

She began flipping burgers, realizing immediately as they fell apart that it was too soon. A bratwurst rolled toward the edge, and she grabbed it with her fingers, burning her knuckles on the grill in the process.

"Ow!" she cried, sticking her fingers into her mouth and sucking them.

"Still haven't learned to cook, have you?"

It was John, and if he wasn't smiling, at least some of the coldness had vanished from his eyes.

"Well, if it isn't the prodigal chef," Rachel said tartly. She handed over the spatula, and he took her place. Still, she didn't leave.

"What do you do, eat in restaurants every night?" he asked, expertly corralling the errant bratwurst.

"A lot of the time," she admitted. "But I did learn to make a few essentials like oatmeal and grilled-cheese sandwiches because of David." *Our son.*

"Those are your two specialties?" he asked distastefully.

"I look upon defrosting as an art," she retorted. "The grocery-store freezer case is my best friend."

He did manage to smile a bit then, and Rachel felt nearly as giddy as she had over ten years ago. But the smile was gone as quickly as it had appeared.

"Go get me the barbecue sauce on the stove," he ordered. "These will be ready in ten minutes."

She didn't object to the order. After all, he was doing the cooking. The least she could do was fetch.

John's mother, Elizabeth, was inside the big pine-paneled kitchen, stirring something sweet and pungent in a huge skillet. She came to Rachel the minute she saw her, hugging her hard.

"I heard you were back," she said, holding Rachel away and smiling. "It's good to see you here again."

"It's nice to be back," Rachel replied warmly. It wasn't quite the truth, but it wasn't the time to tell Elizabeth that her son was making Rachel's return more difficult than she'd anticipated.

"Here, Meredith, stir the German potato salad," Elizabeth said, handing over the spoon to a sullen Meredith. She took Rachel by the shoulders and guided her to a chair at the pine kitchen table, taking the seat opposite. "Now tell me how you're doing. You're not feeling well, are you?'' she demanded before giving Rachel a chance to respond.

"Just a cold," Rachel said. "Nothing serious." From the corner of her eye she could see three men she didn't know opening bags of potato chips and dumping them into bowls while they kept avid ears on her conversation with Elizabeth. Levee workers, she assumed. Meredith was openly listening, as well.

"Do you have any medicine?"

"I haven't had time," Rachel said. "I'm not settled in yet."

"And your son? How's he? I hear he'll be coming for a visit."

"As soon as soccer camp ends, the family he's staying with is putting him on an airplane."

"Wonderful." Elizabeth beamed. "I can't wait to see him."

Both turned as they heard John bellow Rachel's name.

"The barbecue sauce," Rachel said. "I take it he's ready for it."

Elizabeth grinned. "Better hurry, then. John's the impatient one of the lot." As Rachel grasped the handle of the pan with a pot holder, Elizabeth reached into a cupboard and said, "Take this with you. It'll help that cold."

Rachel thanked her for the bottle of cold medication, stuffed it into her pants pocket and started out the door as John bellowed her name again.

"For heaven's sake, hold your horses," Rachel said, frowning at him as she set the pan on the tray.

"I hope you set the table faster than you carry barbecue sauce," he grumbled.

"I was talking to your mother. And I'm not setting the table for you, too." She looked away, then down at the ground uncomfortably.

"Well, what is it?" he growled, brushing sauce on the meat.

"John, I don't know how to say this, but...the way your mother was treating me, the way everyone else is treating me..."

His hands stilled, but he didn't look at her.

"You didn't tell anyone else about what happened between us, did you? About how...bitter the breakup was."

It pained her to ask, and she knew it pained him to answer.

"Do you think I'd take any pleasure in telling others what we said to each other?" he demanded harshly. His eyes swooped to hers, the blue glittering with a hot, angry brilliance. "You were very clear about what you thought of me."

"I was young," she said quietly. "If you remember, I had a temper."

"Had?"

"John, please..."

It was Jordan who interrupted, breaking the tension. "Hey, when are we going to eat?" he asked impatiently, loping toward them from the porch.

"Tell everyone to come sit down," John said, still looking at Rachel's face. "The meat's almost done."

Rachel spun away from John, unwilling to endure the coldness in his face any longer. Her emotions were churning, and she hardly noticed the people beginning to mill around the back of the house. She helped Elizabeth carry out bowls of potato salad and beans and chips without conscious thought.

She deliberately avoided looking at John, but she knew where he was every minute. It was as though she could feel his blame as a physical presence.

Rachel joined the line of ten or so people helping themselves to the food, her eyes cast down. Right now she wished she'd stayed home. She couldn't take much more of John's anger.

There was some space beside Mason at one of the picnic tables, and Rachel sat down there.

Jake and Jordan sat across from her, their plates piled high with food. "I'm ravenous," Jordan complained. "I must have tossed a thousand sandbags today."

"You ate about that many sandwiches, too," Jake said dryly. "Amazing appetite."

"Hard work, brother," Jordan replied, grinning.

"Sandbaggers have it easy, right, Rachel?" Jake said with a wink in her direction. "It's poor carpenters and financial advisors who expend all the mental effort."

"Yeah," Jordan agreed with a lift of his brows. "I can see it has given you some thick muscle between your ears." He jabbed his brother with his elbow, and Jake laughed.

Rachel's smile died as John pushed his way between her and Mason, making himself a place to sit that wasn't there a minute ago. "Great barbecue, wouldn't you say?" John said to his brothers.

"Well, you didn't catch anything on fire, so I suppose it's a success," Jake commented, and Jordan hooted.

"Yeah, like the time you caught Elizabeth's favorite pot holder on fire, the one she won at the church picnic," Mason added.

"It wasn't on fire," John protested. "It was only smoking a little."

"It damn near exploded when you dumped your beer on it," Jordan observed, and the table burst into laughter.

Rachel realized that only Mason wasn't laughing, and a moment later he slid off the seat and quietly walked away. Jake glanced after him, then exchanged a look with John.

That look was too much for Rachel. Mason was her brother, after all. John and his brothers seemed to know what was going on with Mason, and no one was telling her.

With a pointed glare at John, she got up and walked in the direction Mason had gone. She found him at the side of the house, sitting on the concrete cistern top that was practically hidden by a row of forsythia bushes. He was chewing a stalk of grass.

"Hey," she said, plopping down beside him.

"Hey, yourself."

"This is cold on the butt," she complained.

Mason shrugged, and Rachel gave him a punch on the arm. "What's going on with you, Mason?" she asked. "If something's wrong, I want to help."

"This doesn't have anything to do with you." He still wouldn't look at her.

"I'm your sister. Anything that bothers you bothers me." She sighed. "Probably the same stuff bothers you and me, anyway. Mom isn't an easy family history to carry around."

"One difference," Mason said. "You got out of town. Me, I'm stuck here with all the people who remember her— or hold a grudge against her."

Rachel smiled wryly. "How long's she been gone now, thirteen years? People have long memories."

"Do you think there's something to this stuff about genetics?" Mason asked after a bit.

"Why? Are you thinking of taking up the seduction of married women?"

"No," Mason said derisively. "I mean, she used to party pretty heavily."

Rachel frowned. "What are you worried about, Mason? What else happened with the tavern?"

"Nothing." Throwing down the blade of grass, Mason pushed to his feet and strode off, his hands jammed into his pockets.

She'd certainly hit a nerve there, she thought, closing her eyes tightly.

When she opened them, John was standing in front of her. She had to look up to see his face, and he was frowning.

Rachel sighed. More problems. "I was just leaving," she said, starting to stand.

"Wait."

She sat as John lowered himself next to her. He didn't say anything for a long minute, and Rachel sighed again.

"Mason was more talkative than you are," she complained.

"What did he say?"

Rachel shrugged. "I think he's worried that he's turning out like Mom. At least that was the gist of it."

"It wasn't easy for you kids, growing up with your mom and her reputation." John leaned forward and rested his forearms on his knees. "How did you get through it, Rachel?"

"I had you." She turned her head and met his eyes. John looked down.

"Today has been hard for Mason," John said after a short silence. He was trying not to look at her. Every time he looked into those wide, green eyes he saw the past. He saw how things had been between them and how they turned out.

"Why?" she asked.

"Did you know that Mason had a drinking problem?"

"A drinking problem?" Rachel knitted her hands together in her lap and stared at John. "I know he used to have some drinking bouts after his...business setbacks. He didn't seem to have too much trouble getting back on track."

"The bouts got closer together. This time he realized he couldn't stop the way he had all the times before. He's getting some help, and he's been off alcohol for two weeks now. Today's tough because there's beer here for the guys who worked on the levee. Mason hasn't had to be around it until now."

"It must be rough on him," she said, her hands tightening.

"He thinks he's disappointed you," John replied.

"But how could he think that?" Rachel asked, nearly jumping to her feet in agitation.

"Because you left Pierce and you made something of yourself."

"But that's idiotic!"

"It doesn't matter. That's what Mason thinks."

Rachel did climb to her feet then. "I've got to talk to him."

John grabbed her wrist and hauled her back down. "Let him be, Rachel. Jake's talking to him."

"Jake?" She was trying to register John's words, but the touch of his hand on her skin was causing flutters in her chest.

"I guess you didn't know. Jake was married a few years ago while you were gone. His wife and their unborn child were killed in a car accident, and Jake started drinking heavily. It took him a long time to pull himself together. He knows what Mason's going through right now."

"I'm sorry," Rachel said. "I didn't know."

She thought of the McClennon boys' flaming youth, and it made her sad. They'd seen so much trouble since then. John's grip on her wrist had become an unconscious caress, but Rachel didn't move to break the contact.

"What are you thinking about?" he asked.

"You and Jake when you were kids," she said. "The trouble you got into." She smiled gently. "The way you two used to carry on. Jake didn't want you trailing after him, but you went anyway. And you had to do whatever he did. Like the time the two of you snuck into Mrs. Patterson's garden, picked her tomatoes and replaced them with red Christmas tree balls."

John laughed softly. "We had to mow her grass for free all summer as punishment for that one."

"And you'd ride your bikes over the bridge to Missouri to buy fireworks in the summer and shoot them off here on the cistern."

"Seems to me that you were involved in that every year," John reminded her.

"You corrupted me," she teased him. She could remember shooting off the last of their bottle rockets one year and both of them standing here in the dark with sparklers. John had turned to her, smiling, and the next thing either of them knew he was kissing her. It was their first kiss, and it had overwhelmed her senses so much that she singed her hand on the sparkler. John had rubbed cold water on it, then kissed her again.

Now she could see the same memory in his eyes. The hand at her wrist tightened, and his other hand reached out tentatively, halting and then gently touching her face.

Rachel held her breath as John turned her face to his. He studied her seriously a moment, drawn to her almost against his will.

John couldn't stop this any more than he could stop breathing. He had to taste her again, feel her pliant mouth beneath his. Old memories were dragging him toward her, tantalizing and irresistible.

Rachel was leaning into him, apparently drawn by the same unseen force. Her breasts brushed his chest ever so lightly, but the contact was electric for him, making his breath catch in his throat. His hand slid to her hair, holding her still as his mouth softly brushed hers, seeking, asking.

She groaned, straining toward him, and John brought his mouth down on hers with full force. She was even more delicate and more arousing than the dream he'd carried around in his head, and he felt intoxicated.

He lifted his mouth long enough to say her name, and in that one word she heard all the anguish and regret of eleven years. She would have answered him, but his lips pressed hard against hers again, and she opened her own lips in response.

She was lost, melting under his touch, when his head lifted.

Swiftly he drew away, swearing, leaving Rachel desolate and confused.

As they stared at each other, lost in eleven-year-old memories, the first raindrops began to fall. John's eyes flew to the skies, and he swore again, jumping to his feet and pulling Rachel with him.

He began to run toward the house, dragging Rachel behind him.

It was raining harder and faster by the moment. John saw
his brothers and shouted what was on everyone's mind.
"The levee!"

Three

—

Rachel could feel the worry in the kitchen, hanging in the air like smoke from a fire. One face after another turned to John, hard lines etched around each set of eyes.

Elizabeth was adjusting the countertop radio, her expression grim.

"It's moving in from Kansas City," she said. "The weather report says heavy rain with wind."

"It wasn't supposed to get here until tomorrow," John replied wearily.

Jake carried another bowl to the sink. "It seems rain just can't wait to get here this year."

John ran a weary hand through his hair. "All right," he said. "Let's get going."

"I still got the lights in the pickup," Tiny said. "But we're low on sandbags."

"Call the sheriff and tell him we could use another truckload," John told his mother. "And you'd better make some sandwiches for later. All right, let's get going."

The men grabbed light jackets and ponchos from the backs of chairs and headed for the door.

John turned toward the hallway, but Meredith put her hand on his arm. "I'll ride with you," she said.

John shook his head. "You stay here with Rachel and Mom."

Meredith hung back, obviously disappointed, but Rachel followed John to the closet in the hallway.

Out of earshot, she said in a low voice, "I'm going with you."

"Don't be ridiculous," John answered without turning from the closet where he was grabbing extra jackets and caps.

"I mean it, John," Rachel said quietly.

When he faced her, his eyes were cold and distrustful.

"Go home, where you belong."

She knew he meant Boston and not the house on the bluff, but she persisted in the face of his refusal.

"John." She put her hand on his arm. "I can come with you or I can walk to the levee myself. Either way, I'm going to help."

He jerked his arm away as if her touch had burned him through his windbreaker. "What kind of game are you playing, Rachel? How could the levee possibly matter to you?"

"The people who live here matter to me," she said, holding his angry gaze. "I can't just sit idly by without doing anything while they lose their homes."

"It seems to me you didn't care about what people lost in the past," he accused with a deadly calm that belied the fire in his eyes. "You waited until a better deal came along, other obligations be damned."

"That's not fair," she countered. "What happened between you and me has nothing to do with this."

"It has everything to do with this, Rachel," he growled. "I can't trust you. And one thing levee workers need is trust in each other."

"Hey, you coming, John?" a male voice called from the kitchen.

John was silent a moment, his eyes boring into Rachel, before he turned toward the voice. "Yeah, I'm on my way."

Rachel started to hurry after him, but she saw Meredith standing in the doorway. From her surprised expression, Rachel gathered that Meredith had overheard most of the bitter exchange. Meredith flushed and left.

Rachel gritted her teeth and headed resolutely for the kitchen. Meredith was just going out the door, calling for the men to wait for her. Pickup trucks revved their engines in the drive, their windshield wipers working to keep up with the rain. Elizabeth looked up in surprise as Rachel ran for the door.

"You shouldn't be out in the rain with a cold," Elizabeth admonished her, but Rachel was already gone.

She managed to squeeze into the back seat of Tiny's pickup with the elongated cab as he was about to follow the parade of five trucks pulling away. Briefly she nodded to the other two men in the front seat, someone she vaguely remembered who owned a farm downriver and another man she thought she recalled running the local tire store.

"How come John didn't give you one of those ponchos?" Tiny asked worriedly. "What was he thinking about?"

"His mind was on the levee," Rachel lied. She wasn't at all sure that John would give her one of the ponchos when he saw that she'd come along despite his objections. She untied the sweater around her shoulders and slipped into it, a process made more difficult by the cramped quarters in the truck's rear seat.

Tiny was apparently an avid collector of empty peanut-butter jars, because the back seat was littered with them, along with a year's collection of farming magazines and extension service publications.

"Sorry about the mess," he said apologetically, glancing in the rearview mirror. "I eat peanut butter when I'm plowing or running into town, and it just seemed easier to leave the peanut butter in the truck." He shrugged and grinned. "Saves a few steps to the house."

"But what do you spread it on?" Rachel couldn't help wondering.

"Crackers," Tiny said. "Should be some back there. Go ahead and help yourself."

Rachel graciously passed on the offer, and Tiny warmed to the subject of food.

"I keep those magazines because they've got a new recipe every week," he said. "Going to learn to cook someday."

"It won't happen in my lifetime," one of the other men snorted.

"I don't know," Rachel said. "Maybe we'll learn together, Tiny."

"Hey, yeah," Tiny responded enthusiastically. "Maybe John'll send us both to cooking school."

He exchanged a meaningful look with the man next to him, leaving Rachel to conclude what they were thinking. They imagined that John would take up with her again now that she was here. But nothing could be further from the truth. He wasn't likely to send her to cooking school or any other school, with the possible exception of a school of sharks.

Rachel braced herself inwardly when they reached the levee. When John found out she was here, no doubt everyone would be treated to a display of just what he thought of her.

It didn't matter, though. She had to be here, whether John David McClennon liked it or not.

She didn't have to wait long for his reaction. Steely blue eyes swung to her the instant she stepped from the truck, despite the fact that she'd tried to minimize her presence by sticking close behind Tiny and the two others. She knew she was hiding, but she needed all the help she could get.

"I thought I told you to stay at the house," John barked as he swung a box of battery-operated lanterns to the ground, then stalked toward her.

The rain was pelting her, making her hair cling to her face and her shoulders hunch involuntarily, but she wouldn't back down. It was a cold rain for June, and she tried hard not to shiver.

"I'm here now, so you'd better make the best of it," she snapped.

"John, you know what I think—" Tiny began in a conciliatory voice.

"I think you'd better stay out of this, Tiny," John growled.

Tiny cleared his throat, then apparently thought better of any further heroics. With a clumsy pat on Rachel's shoulder, he moved to the back of his truck to unload.

"You have any more knights in shining armor ready to take up your cause?" John asked sarcastically. He had stopped only a couple of feet from her, and his physical presence was intimidating enough without his barbs.

"I don't need any," she snapped. "I've learned to take care of myself."

"So I see," he said with a derisive look at her bedraggled appearance. She was getting wetter by the moment—and more uncomfortable.

"Have you had enough fun?" she finally demanded in irritation. "Because if you have, I'll start sandbagging."

She turned away bitterly, but John caught her arm, spinning her back to him.

"The ponchos are on the front seat of my truck," he said without emotion. "This is hard work. Try not to hurt yourself."

He turned away before she could make any other retort and went back to unloading lanterns. There was a little light left from the setting sun, though it was a murky light with the rain, so she supposed the men expected to work well into the dark.

She realized that she was truly shivering now, her skin soaked and cold except for the place where John had grabbed her arm. That was warm.

Rachel lowered her head briefly as she leaned into John's truck to pull out a poncho. She had never thought that facing John again would be so difficult. She felt drained, physically and emotionally, and she'd spent less than half a day with him.

It was just because she was sick with a cold, she told herself. She was worn-out and ill-equipped to withstand John's barbs and icy stares.

"Are you all right?" a worried voice asked behind her.

She straightened too quickly, bumping her head on the top of the car. "Ow!" She rubbed her head and tried to smile at Tiny. "Yes, I'm okay. It's just that John and I..." She let the words trail off, deciding it was better to leave all of that alone. There was speculation enough without her adding to it by discussing her woes.

"Yeah," Tiny said after a bit. "I noticed. He can be a bear when he's irritated." He frowned. "Maybe you ought to stay in the truck or let me take you home, Rachel. You're looking a bit peaked."

She shook her head. "I'll be all right. I just need to work the kinks out."

She put on the poncho, grateful that at last the rain wasn't running down the back of her neck. Living in the city, she had forgotten how it was to be caught out in the rain in an open field.

Giving Tiny a reassuring smile, she moved to help the men unload sandbags from the truck. But this section of field brought back memories. She and John had been caught in the rain more than once here.

Rachel had always trailed after John, begging him to let her help him with the farm chores. Usually he relented after fifteen minutes of her pestering and gave her some menial task that made her happy. All she really wanted was to be near him.

She had gradually learned to do many of the necessities around a farm, but still John would tease her about not knowing what she was doing.

She was sixteen, and he was home from college for the summer. She trailed after him as persistent as ever. By now she was in love with John David McClennon.

He had teased her endlessly as she trudged through the field, following him while he checked his corn. It was cloudy and the temperature was dropping, bringing needed relief from the heat. She had finally had enough of his teasing. She'd stalked away angrily, intending to go home. John had run after her, calling her name and apologizing.

She wouldn't listen, and he grabbed her arm as he'd done today, spinning her around to him.

Rachel had landed against his chest. They both froze. Then John's mouth had come down on hers, hard, and Rachel felt that at that moment she'd had everything she needed in life.

"Rachel, those are too heavy for you," Tiny admonished now, and she came back to the present with a start. She was holding a sandbag and heading for the pile next to the levee.

She wasn't sure how many she had carried in her reverie, but her arms felt as though it had been more than a few.

"I'm fine, Tiny," she assured him, moving on. From the corner of her eye she saw John watching her, his frown still firmly in place. She dropped the sandbag and started back for another.

"Here, Rachel, let's start a line," Tiny said at her shoulder.

Soon they were tossing the sandbags from one to another down the line until the last person deposited them on the growing pile. Looking at the ground by the levee, Rachel supposed that it was too wet to drive the pickup closer. She also saw Meredith at the end of the line next to John.

John and his needy women, she thought sadly. None of us can help ourselves from falling all over him. He should start a retirement home for us where we can sigh over him and pass our days with memories.

* * *

They had sandbagged for well over four hours, using every sandbag they had brought and half of those the sheriff delivered two hours before. Rachel worked automatically, ignoring her sore back and wet feet. She listened to the men talk about the other levees. The Curtis farm was in danger, they were saying. Floodwater was seeping around sandbags at the Curtises' front yard. It would enter the house shortly if not stopped.

Curtis. The name was so familiar. Memory struck Rachel like a blow. Norma Curtis. She was Norma Cline when she went to school with Rachel, but she had married Eric Curtis.

Rachel had always liked Norma. When they were in school together, Norma was always kind to her. With John away at college, it was Norma who had helped Rachel get Mason home when he went on one of his drinking binges.

Rachel jumped when a hand landed heavily on her shoulder. She recognized John's face in the lantern light, and for a moment time seemed to slip away.

"The rain stopped, Rachel," he said gruffly. "Go on home."

She stared up at the sky in wonder. A sliver of moon shone through the haze, glancing off the three-foot pile of sandbags on the levee. Beyond the pile, she could hear the river, turbulent and angry.

"Where is everybody?" she asked, looking around.

"They're leaving to get some sleep. Go on. Tiny's waiting for you."

She saw that the other pickups were pulling slowly away, and she let the sandbag she was holding drop to the ground. Every muscle ached, but all she could think about was how much would be lost if even one levee gave way.

For some reason, it was important that she see Norma.

"Rachel!" John said sharply when she turned toward the remaining truck. His hands sought her face and tilted it up. "You've been coughing the last couple of hours. You need to get some rest."

"It's just a cold," she said. The humidity had seeped through her clothes, making her hot and sticky and uncomfortable.

"Go on up to my house," he said. "The cabin's no place for you tonight."

"I don't want to put your mother out," she said quietly.

"Mom won't be there."

Rachel stared at him, not understanding.

"She moved into an apartment in town a couple of years ago when her arthritis got bad. She can't climb stairs well, anymore."

"You live alone?"

"I can't seem to keep a woman," he said dryly. His hands dropped from her face. His eyes probed hers a moment longer before he said, "Go on. You need the rest."

Rachel shook her head. "I'll stay at the cabin."

"Don't be stupid, Rachel."

His voice had taken on an angry tone again, but Rachel turned toward Tiny's truck. "I'll be all right."

"You always are, aren't you?" he demanded coldly from behind her, but Rachel kept walking.

He could have kicked himself after she was gone. He'd had nothing for her but harsh words even after all the work she'd done tonight. He knew she wouldn't take care of herself the way she should. He should have gotten her home himself and made sure she took a hot bath and got a good night's sleep.

But thoughts of Rachel in the bath only deviled him more than his conscience already had. Cursing, he brought his fist down on the top of his pickup. Why did she have to come back here and make him remember things he'd put behind him long ago?

He didn't even dream about her anymore, not after he learned that working from sunup to sundown and falling into bed exhausted was the quickest way to wipe out dreams.

And now she was back.

He was just going to have to deal with it until she left again. Because Rachel Tucker was sure to leave sooner or later. She'd never be happy here, especially with him around. He could almost promise her that.

It was an hour later when Rachel found the Curtises' house and pulled her rental car into the long drive. Her headlights pierced the mist enough to see the encroaching water at the back of the house. A few people were working by the light of truck headlights, adding sandbags to a pile that defined the perimeter of the backyard. Already water was breaching the top.

Norma was in the yard pouring coffee for the workers, and she turned at the sound of the car door.

"Rachel? Rachel, is that really you?" she said, quickly setting down the pot and launching herself at Rachel.

They hugged long and hard, unconstrained by the crowd that went on working.

"Is there anything I can do?" Rachel asked helplessly.

Norma sighed and tightened her arm on Rachel's shoulder. "Think you could pour some coffee and make sandwiches for a while? I'm too keyed up to sleep, but I'd love to get off my feet for a little bit."

"What about the sandbagging?" Rachel suggested. "Should I do that instead?"

"No, but thanks. We've got so many people here that they're running into each other. Now that the rain's stopped we might be able to keep the water out another night, anyway." She glanced back at her house.

"Did you get everything out?" Rachel asked, filling coffee mugs as workers approached her.

"All the essentials. We almost took the cabinets off the wall, too, but, hell, I've been wanting new ones."

"If you were thinking, Norma, you would have left your clothes instead."

Norma laughed. "A whole new wardrobe! Lord, I haven't been clothes shopping in ages. Other than for this one," she added as a boy who looked to be about eight dashed up to her with an important request for more sandwiches.

"I'll get them," Rachel said, waving Norma back to her seat.

"This is Eric, Junior," Norma said, pulling the bashful boy forward. "Eric, I went to high school with Rachel Tucker. You be nice to her now, because she's a rich banker." The last was said in a stage whisper, making Rachel and the boy grin.

When Eric had run back to the crew with a plate of sandwiches, Norma gestured Rachel to a lawn chair beside her and said, "How's your little boy doing, Rachel?"

"David's fine," Rachel told her. "He'll be here as soon as he finishes soccer camp."

There was a long silence before Norma asked, "How are things between you and John?"

"I doubt that they could get much worse," Rachel admitted ruefully. "He's barely civil to me."

"There never was any other woman for John but you, not even Meredith. She pushed him into marriage. He's never gotten over you, Rachel."

Rachel was glad the darkness hid the flush on her face as she remembered the way John had kissed her.

"I think he's a lonely man who could break a woman's heart if she let him," she said honestly.

And he would probably enjoy breaking hers after what had happened between them eleven years ago.

"And, knowing you, you're determined not to give him the chance. Listen, Rachel—"

"I can't afford to listen, Norma," Rachel interrupted. "I can't afford to listen to anything but common sense. And common sense tells me to stay as far from John McClennon as I can get."

"Rachel, you don't know what John's been like these past few years. If you'd seen the way he sits in silence for hours, the way he never smiles, it would make you cry."

"He had Meredith," Rachel objected, refusing to be moved by John's isolation.

"She isn't you, and she's the first to realize it," Norma snorted.

"Well, I can't do anything about that," Rachel said wearily. "And I can't change what happened in the past."

"I suppose you know best," Norma said grudgingly, but she didn't sound at all convinced. "Well, come on. Tell me all about your exciting life."

Rachel hadn't slept well in the cabin. It wasn't just because she wasn't used to the bed or there were unfamiliar night sounds. It was the memories of John that chased sleep away.

She was over him, she told herself. This was just a temporary reaction brought on by fatigue and her cold.

Before going to bed she'd taken a healthy teaspoonful of the medicine Elizabeth had given her, and she felt a little better despite her sleeplessness. Her cough was still bad, though, making her lean on the kitchen counter when it took over.

Rachel was pouring a second cup of coffee when she heard the truck door slam and then some kind of quiet argument outside her door. She didn't want to be caught standing in her short, flannel nightshirt, especially not by John. She was about to hightail it back to the bedroom when the door opened without preliminaries and John walked in, followed by his mother. Both carried pails and cleaning supplies.

John was apparently as paralyzed as she was when he caught sight of her frozen in mid-sip at the counter. Elizabeth nearly collided with his back.

"I *told* you to knock first," Elizabeth chastised him. "I told him to knock first," she repeated to Rachel, shaking her head as she made her way around her son, who was still as unmoving as a statue.

Only his eyes betrayed the emotion he was feeling. Rachel could feel their censure from across the room.

Elizabeth looked from Rachel to John, giving John a clear signal with her eyes that perhaps he should stop staring at Rachel. But John seemed oblivious to all signals.

Flushing, Rachel hurriedly set down the cup and headed for the bedroom.

She closed the door, then sat down on the bed, giving in to a fit of coughing before she summoned her energy to change clothes.

In the kitchen, Elizabeth scanned John's face the way she had done when he had gotten himself into trouble as a little boy. But he wouldn't look at her, instead he busied himself at the kitchen sink.

"You haven't said anything about how you feel about Rachel being back," she said in a quiet voice as she came to stand beside him.

"How should I feel?" he demanded, banging his wrenches down with unnecessary force. He looked darkly at the closed bedroom door.

"I don't know," Elizabeth said. "But it's worth talking about."

"No," John said, beginning to remove the rusty kitchen faucet. "There's nothing worth talking about. Rachel will be gone soon, and we can get on with our lives."

"Is that what you want?" his mother asked, handing him a different wrench. "It seems to me you're unhappy when she's gone, and you're unhappy when she's here."

"I'll be less unhappy when she's gone," he said dryly.

"Are you sure?" his mother persisted, tilting her head up to see into his face.

His hands finally stilled, his head bending slightly to look at her. "No, Mom," he said in a grating whisper. "I'm not. And that's the hell of it."

They both looked around as Rachel came out of the bedroom. She had put on an old pair of jeans and a gray sweatshirt. She had brushed the tangles from her hair. But her green eyes looked far too large and feverish against her pale skin.

"Are you all right?" John demanded, setting down the wrench and walking toward her.

Rachel nodded and turned away from him. She was tired and still not feeling well, but she didn't want him to know.

Despite the warm day, she was fighting off shivers. But if she couldn't keep pace with him and his mother, he would surely say something about it. She wasn't sure which would hurt more, his anger that she hadn't gotten the sleep she needed or his derision that she wasn't pulling her own weight.

Rachel ignored the silence behind her as she rooted through the small closet off the bedroom for the cleaning things George and Rowena had always kept there. She found an old sponge and a bottle of all-purpose cleaner and set to work on the small bathroom. The floor was filthy, and she got down on her hands and knees, scrubbing hard. The exertion made her cough, so she quietly closed the bathroom door to keep John from hearing.

But the door kept out little sound, and as she worked, she listened to Elizabeth trying to make small talk with John with no apparent success.

She really hadn't expected things to be this bad between her and John. She had just assumed that the passage of time would ease whatever anger and pain he had felt at her betrayal. She hadn't counted on John's unforgiving heart. He seemed determined to make her pay for the past.

As if she hadn't paid enough, she thought. She had raised their son alone, emotionally and financially, despite her fear that she would turn out to be as poor a mother as her own. And when David had asked about his father, she'd said that he would meet him when the time was right.

Who was she trying to fool? There was never going to be a right time. There was none eleven years ago, and there was none now.

John's voice behind her made her jump. "A sponge won't do much good on that tile. I'll get some of Mom's scouring pads."

His frown deepened when she turned to look at him over her shoulder.

"I think you're running a fever," he said, squatting beside her and pressing one large hand to her forehead.

"I'm just hot from working," she said. She realized she must be very hot, indeed, because his hand felt like ice against her temples.

"What are you trying to prove?" he demanded, jerking away his hand.

"I don't know what you mean, John," she said wearily, tiring of their fight before it even started.

John grasped her shoulders and stood, pulling her up with him. He took the sponge from her fingers and threw it on the floor. "Are you trying to kill yourself in front of me?" he said roughly. "You're obviously sick."

"If I'd wanted to kill myself in front of you, I would have chosen a more dramatic time," she stormed, her own anger taking over. "Like your wedding."

She was instantly sorry she'd said it, but it was too late to call the words back.

"Why would it matter to you if I married, when you had your own lover, a lover you obviously preferred over me?" His hands tightened on her shoulders, but she welcomed the pressure. It kept her from saying too much. It had nearly killed her to discover that while she carried his child, he had married someone else.

"It didn't matter," she mumbled. She desperately sought a way to turn the conversation in another direction. "I need a cup of tea," she said suddenly. It was an inane change of topic, but it apparently worked. His eyes no longer probed hers with such insistence.

"I'll get it," he volunteered. "Go lie down and get some rest."

She was too tired to push him anymore, so she did what he said.

She kicked off her shoes and lay down on the bed, more tired than she could remember. She must have dozed off immediately, because she woke to the sound of the kettle whistling in the kitchen. A minute later John came in with a mug in his hand.

He sat on the edge of the bed, his eyes refusing to meet hers despite his nearness.

"Thank you," she said politely, sitting up and taking the mug carefully to avoid his fingers.

"You're not coughing now," he observed.

"I know," she said. "I took another teaspoon of the medicine your mother gave me."

His eyes moved to the bottle of medicine on the bedside table and then to the picture propped up beside it. "Is this your son?" he asked, taking the picture and studying it.

"Yes. David." Her hands tightened around the mug.

"He's a good-looking boy."

Like his father. He had Rachel's blond hair, but John's blue eyes.

"He loves sports," she said, smiling tightly. "And animals. He's been pestering me to get him a dog."

"You can have dogs in your apartment?" he asked, his eyes swinging to her face.

She was so animated when she talked about her son, he thought. And so fearful when she found him looking at her. He didn't ever want her to fear him, but he supposed he'd given her plenty of reason with his anger.

His mother was right. He didn't know what he wanted where Rachel was concerned. He was going to be miserable whether she came into his life or went out of it.

"No," she said, shaking her head. "No pets."

"Then you should move. A boy who wants a dog should have one."

It was true. It was part of the reason she was moving back here, to give David the things that were important in life. And maybe to give him his father. A chill chased through her as a horrible thought came to her. What if John didn't want his son any more than he wanted Rachel? She couldn't bear the thought of John taking out his anger on David. It would break her heart.

"What's wrong?" He was frowning as he took the mug of tea from her. He set it on the table and felt her forehead again. "You're still hot."

"I just need some rest," she said, wishing she could lie back and feel his hands touching her all over the way they had in the past. She was almost ashamed of the thought, but not quite. It had been a long drought without love for her, and she couldn't help wanting it.

"You shouldn't have gone to the Curtises' place last night," he said, almost reluctantly, she thought.

"You know about that?" She was nearly incredulous that he wasn't furious with her.

"Of course I know," he said dryly. "Do you think you can go anywhere in this county without someone telling me about it? 'Rachel was in buying groceries. Rachel was driving down Main Street. Rachel was visiting with Norma Curtis last night.' That's all I hear, scouting reports on your activities."

The teasing frustration in his voice made her smile. "I didn't know I was such a topic of interest," she said.

"Oh, but you are. Just like the old days. Everyone seems to think we're an item."

"I guess they'll have to get used to the idea that we're not," she said, surprised that her voice wasn't wavering.

"Yes," he agreed. "But I'm sure it will become clear to them when you leave here."

She didn't say anything about that, unsure how he would take the news that she was staying. "I thought you'd be angry that I went to see Norma last night."

"I'm not too happy about it in light of the fact that you're sick," he said. "But old friends are what's important around here. I would have done the same thing myself."

She and John weren't even old friends anymore, she thought sadly.

"How's their levee holding today?" she asked.

"All right, so far. They're still pumping out some overflow, but it looks like it's slowed down."

"Good." She nodded, satisfied for the moment.

John still held the photo of their son in his hand, and she couldn't help looking at it and thinking how much David was like his father had been at that age.

"What is his—David's—father like?" John asked, making her start as if he'd read her mind. He reached out absently to brush a strand of hair from her forehead.

"He's a very kind man," she said honestly, meeting his eyes.

"And this kind man didn't marry you?" John asked harshly.

"It wasn't right for either of us," she said, her eyes sliding away.

"And what about David? What's right for him?"

"David's happy," she hedged.

"Happy without a father?" he persisted. "How often does he see his father?"

"He doesn't," she admitted wearily.

"Why not?"

"It just hasn't worked out," she said evasively. "I don't speak to his father."

"Hasn't worked out?" he exploded. "Rachel, what kind of man doesn't see his own child? Or does he think his money is an even trade?"

"I don't get money from him," she insisted stubbornly.

"I don't understand you," he said, his voice rising again. "You take up with a man because he has financial means, but then you don't even make him support his son. What's happened to you, Rachel?"

What had happened, indeed? she wondered miserably. She had certainly made a mess of this whole thing. Her son had no father, and she had lost her best friend in the whole world.

"Rachel, look at me." His hand lifted her chin up until she met his eyes. She saw the anger there and the disappointment, and her misery deepened. "What you did to the two of us—to me—was pain enough. But how can you hurt your own son by denying him his father?"

"I'm not—" she began, but bit off what she had been about to say, knowing that it wasn't true. It was her fault that David didn't know his father. Tears gathered in her eyes.

"Rachel," he said, shaking his head, "I used to hope that one day you'd realize you'd made a foolish mistake, choosing a man because of money. It looks like you've paid for that mistake. I wish things had been different, but I'm more sorry that your son is still paying."

"John," Elizabeth interrupted from the doorway, "let her rest. She needs to get her strength back."

John nodded without looking at his mother. His hand dropped from Rachel's chin, and he set David's photo on the nightstand. His eyes never left Rachel's.

"Mom's right," he said bitterly as he stepped away from the bed. "You've lost your strength—and your character."

Rachel closed her eyes to stop the tears. His words had stung more than she was willing to let him see. John McClennon had never thought her weak willed and lacking in character in the past. That he would say so now was hard evidence of the harsh judgment he'd made about her.

Taking a deep breath, she opened her eyes to find the door closed and the room empty.

Four

Rachel wasn't sure what time it was when she woke up. The sky was dark, and she could hear raindrops hitting the gutters. *More rain.* Her heart sank.

A steady dripping of water came from her left, and when she rolled over, she saw the ceiling leaking onto the floor. Already, the rotting floorboards were turning dark from the water they'd absorbed.

Rachel grabbed a large pan from the kitchen and stuck it under the leak, then dressed.

She found a note from Elizabeth on the kitchen counter saying that she'd left her a sandwich in the refrigerator. Rachel found an apple and some carrot sticks beside the sandwich, making her smile. Elizabeth had always insisted that the children eat all of their meal before they could have any dessert. The rule stood even when Rachel was visiting, and back then no one loved dessert more than Rachel.

While she was brewing a cup of tea, she found the tin of chocolate-chip cookies hidden in the cupboard. That made her smile all over again.

She sobered when she thought of John. They couldn't be in the same room together without fighting, or striking sparks off each other. She didn't know how it was for him, but when he touched her, she seemed to explode inside into tiny shards of sensation.

The rain sounded as if it was falling harder. She moved to the window with her sandwich, but she couldn't see much through the filmy glass.

She looked at the clock on the counter. It was six in the evening. No doubt John had been hard at work on the levee since the rain started.

Rachel was feeling a lot better, and her cough wasn't as bad. She fidgeted in the cabin after she ate, pacing and making halfhearted attempts to put some things away.

She kept straying to the window, trying to see the levee. She opened the door and listened hard. She could hear real or imagined voices carried on the wind, she wasn't sure which.

These people meant so much to her. The farmers and their wives who hadn't asked questions when things were bad with her mother, who slipped her a five-dollar bill or invited her for dinner when they knew her mother had drunk up all the food money. And when her mother died, they came to her, bringing food and comforting arms.

The salt of the earth. She had once called John that in jest, but it was true. As corny as it sounded, it was true. These were people you could lean on and trust.

She couldn't just sit here in the cabin high above all the danger and wait for the river to swallow their farms and their lives.

Rachel pulled on the poncho John had given her and ran out the door.

She knew the rental car would be practically useless in the mud, so she half walked and half ran toward the levee, sliding down the incline from the bluff and tearing her pants in the process. Her sneakers were already covered in mud, making her wish she'd bought some work boots in town.

But nothing mattered except helping the levee workers.

And seeing John again.

She couldn't stop herself from wanting to be near him, whether he was angry with her or not. Wanting John was like losing control sliding down the bluff; she was unable to slow the momentum and too exhilarated by the slide to care.

Approaching breathlessly, she saw a group of men clustered around a boil in the earth. The water had seeped through beneath the levee and was now perilously close to breaching the surface. The men worked quickly, sealing off the boil with sandbags. John was working at a furious pace, pausing only when someone else called him from farther down the levee.

Rachel ducked deeper into the oversize poncho and hurried to the workers farthest away from him. Tiny raised his head at her approach, his brows shooting up in warning.

"You'd better not let John see you here. He's been barking at all of us like a tall dog on a short leash."

"I plan to stay out of his way," Rachel assured him, hefting one of the sandbags and dropping it on top of the levee. She sucked in her breath in alarm when she saw how close the river had come to topping the wall of sandbags.

"Yeah, it's been gaining on us," Tiny said. "Nothing but rain all month here and up north. All that water just swells the river." He shook his head and went back to work.

Rachel could feel John approaching without having to look. She bent her back, the poncho hood pulled well over her face, and rearranged sandbags. She heard him snap something to Tiny about checking another boil a mile away, and then his footsteps thudded off.

Tiny was right, she thought. John was in a foul mood.

She worked for two hours without encountering John again, her only companions the rhythm of the rain pelting the poncho and the occasional grunts of someone lifting a sandbag. Gradually, her movements became rote as she moved sandbags from the ground to the levee, and she wasn't even aware that dusk was settling over the river.

A truck came to a stop near the levee sometime later, making Rachel look up in surprise as the headlights washed over her. It was night already, and she hadn't noticed. The rain had slowed to a light drizzle some time ago, but still the river relentlessly rose.

Meredith slammed the truck door, straightening her spine when she spotted Rachel.

She handed out buckets of fried chicken to the workers, and when they were absorbed in their meal, she approached Rachel.

"When are you going home?" she asked bluntly.

Rachel didn't pretend that Meredith meant the cabin. "I don't know," she hedged. She'd told no one that she was here to stay, and Meredith didn't seem like a good first choice for the information.

"He's happy with me," Meredith insisted, her hands clenched at her sides, her face earnestly miserable. "It's over for you two."

"Meredith, it's been over for you, as well," Rachel said as gently as she could.

"Oh, we're divorced, but..." She trailed off, and Rachel felt a pang of pity for the woman as she saw the desperation that Meredith couldn't hide. She saw that Meredith knew it was over, too, but as long as there were no rivals for John's affection, she could pretend that it wasn't.

"Meredith, maybe it's time we both got on with our lives," she said.

"It was always you he wanted," Meredith said, her lower lip trembling. "No matter what I did, it was you. At least when you were gone, he noticed me. I just wanted to be with him."

Meredith stopped, her face coloring, and Rachel knew she had said far more than she'd intended.

Rachel didn't know what to tell her. She knew what it was to want badly, only to find out how futile your own want is. She knew how miserable Meredith felt. But she couldn't offer her comfort, because their wants were too inextricably tied.

"Maybe things will work out for the best," she said, knowing that it was little consolation.

Meredith sighed and turned back to the truck without saying another word. It was a sad fact of life, Rachel acknowledged, that loving someone could be as painful as it was intoxicating.

A hard hand clamped down on Rachel's shoulder, making her jump.

"What are you doing here?" John demanded, turning her to face him.

He looked exhausted—and furious.

"I got plenty of sleep," she told him. "I came to help."

"Help?" he repeated sharply, his eyes probing hers relentlessly. He had thrown back his poncho hood, and his dark hair was wet with the rain. Rachel had to curl her fingers at her sides to keep from reaching out to touch it. "We don't need your help, Rachel. Why didn't you just stay in the cabin where you belong?"

"I *can't* stay there while everyone's working! It makes me feel like some stranger, an outsider. These are my friends, too, John."

"Have you asked them if they want your help?" he demanded. "Maybe they feel the same way I do."

It was a cruel barb. She felt the blood drain from her face, but before she could turn away Tiny came running from the levee.

"John! Come quick!"

Alarmed, Rachel stood a moment as John and Tiny raced for the levee. Without thinking, she joined the throng of workers running after John and Tiny. She halted, out of breath, at the pile of sandbags, straining to see around the men in front of her until someone moved aside so she could see.

The Coleman lanterns reflected on the water, gilding the ripples like fine lace. The dark water churned, but as she watched, she could see that the level was dropping.

Silence fell over the crowd.

"I imagine the break's to the north of us," John said wearily.

"We can all get some sleep now," Tiny said. "Though I won't rest easy knowing it comes at the expense of someone else."

There were murmurs of tired assent from the men around Rachel.

"I'll check it out as soon as I get into some dry clothes," John said.

"What happened?" Meredith asked, coming to stand beside John.

"There's been a levee break somewhere else," he said. "That's why the water's dropping here."

"Oh, then we can quit work," Meredith said, brightening.

John's jaw tightened. "Yes, we can quit tonight." He turned toward Rachel, his eyes searching hers, but he wasn't speaking to her. "Go on home, Meredith."

"We could get some dinner," she suggested hopefully.

"I'm not hungry. Go on home."

Rachel waited, knowing this business with John wasn't over. Meredith walked back to her truck slowly, followed by the rest of the workers, their voices low with sadness over the levee break.

Rachel tensed as the last truck began to pull away. She couldn't move from the spot with John's eyes boring into her with angry accusation.

Another truck came slowly across the muddy field, and John turned to look as Mason and Jake got out.

"The break's up at the Cedarwood levee," Jake said. "Mason and I were sandbagging there. It'll all be a lake by morning."

"Did they evacuate before it went?" John asked.

"Everybody got out safely, but the grain elevator and most of the houses are under water now."

John swore. "I don't know how much longer the rest of us can hold out," he said.

There was a long silence.

Jake put his hand on his brother's shoulder. "Go get some rest. Mason and I'll keep an eye on things here. We got some sleep in Cedarwood when the sheriff brought some inmates to spell us for a while."

"All right." John still watched Rachel, making her wonder how much longer she could meet his gaze without looking away.

"I'm going to go sleep, too," she said as Jake and Mason moved down the levee.

She'd only taken a step when John caught her arm and turned her to him. "Is the cabin roof leaking?" he challenged.

Rachel drew a shaky breath, trying to ignore the hand on her wrist. "Yes."

He abruptly released her, as if he'd been waiting for that answer. "Go sleep at my house tonight."

"I put a pan under the leak," she said flatly. "It won't be a problem." She tried to leave again and heard him swear behind her.

"Those floorboards are rotten already," he called to her back. "And God knows how much longer that ceiling will hold before it falls in."

She kept walking toward the bluff without answering.

"You don't mean to tell me you *walked* here and you're walking home?" he demanded.

"I walk farther than that when I go grocery shopping," she informed him without turning around.

"And that's after sitting at a desk all day, not lifting sandbags in the rain. Look at you! You're wet and tired and sick. Have you lost your mind, Rachel?"

No, she thought, *but I wish to heaven I would so I wouldn't think about you every waking minute.*

She heard his truck door slam and then the whine of the motor and thud of tires bumping over mud. The sound came toward her. She kept walking as the truck drew up alongside.

"Get in," he said quietly. "I can't stand to watch you kill yourself trying to prove something."

It was his tone that persuaded her. The old gentleness was there, so much so that she almost burst into tears.

Rachel walked to the passenger's side and climbed in, realizing how cold, wet and weary she really was. She probably wouldn't have made it halfway back up the hill to the cabin. She leaned back against the seat, shivering, and let her eyes close.

It seemed only seconds later that John stopped the truck in front of his house.

"Come on," he coaxed her, coming around to open her door and help her slide down from the seat. He walked her to the door, his arm enfolded around her shoulders, holding her against him.

The scent of coffee and lilacs enveloped her as she walked inside, making her smile. "Flowers," she murmured. "Your house always smelled of flowers."

"That's Mom's doing," he said. "She was always the family gardener. She still insists on bringing flowers over here every week." He steered her toward the stairs. "Though no one's around to enjoy them."

"My shoes," she protested before John could escort her off the hallway carpet.

He knelt and pulled off her muddy sneakers, frowning up at her as he saw how wet she was despite the poncho.

It made her sad to think of John here alone. She sighed heavily as they started up the stairs, and that precipitated a fit of coughing.

"You're going to have pneumonia," he chided her. "I've never met anyone as stubborn as you, Rachel Tucker."

Or as beautiful. Or as beguiling. Touching her like this was making him remember so many other times, so many feelings that he'd buried after that phone call all those years ago.

He'd never wanted her to suffer any of the hurts she'd endured on account of her mother. He'd wanted to protect her and keep her happy. He was furious and in pain himself when she left him for someone else—the pain doubled by the knowledge it was someone who could give her things he couldn't—but he felt a strange sense of comfort that at least she would be happy.

But she wasn't happy now. She was no more happy than he was.

Rachel hesitated momentarily at the bedroom doorway. It was John's room. They'd made love there once on a hot summer night with the breeze from the open window playing over them.

But the room looked as though it hadn't been slept in for a long time now. Linens and storage boxes were piled on the bed.

"I sleep in the other room," John said as if reading her mind. He began to clear the bed. "The bathroom is through there. It's the only one with a shower, so if you don't mind I'll shower there in the morning."

She quickly shook her head. "No, that's fine." He was treating her as if she'd never been in this house, as if they were acquaintances and not once friends and lovers.

The bed cleared, he stood back.

"That dresser has some of my old things you can wear," he said, pointing to the walnut marble-top dresser with the oval mirror she'd loved so much. The morning after they'd made love, she'd stood there in front of that mirror with John behind her, his arms encircling her, his cheek resting on her head.

Rachel had been home from college, and John was taking over the farming after his father's death. That particular day Elizabeth had been out of town, and John and Rachel had the house to themselves. Everything had been right with the world that morning. Now, nothing seemed right anymore.

"Get out of those wet clothes," he said. "I'll bring you some hot tea."

He was gone the next minute, closing the door behind him and leaving Rachel to stand in the middle of the room shivering and sad.

She opened the top drawer of the dresser and rummaged through John's cast-off T-shirts. Most had holes, and all were faded, but she came up with a large white one that was clean and still intact. Slipping into the adjoining bathroom, she hastily discarded her wet clothes and pulled on the T-shirt. It came almost to her knees.

It still smelled faintly of the soap John had always used, and that made her want to cry all over again.

She was standing in front of the mirror, toweling her hair when he tapped on the door.

Pulling down the T-shirt as far as it would go, she called for him to come in.

John looked at her a moment before his eyes slid away. "Here," he said, setting the cup of tea on the night table beside the bed. "Do you need anything else?"

Rachel shook her head. She was holding the towel clutched to her chest, and she couldn't stop looking at John's face, at the worry lines around his mouth and the loneliness in his eyes. How he must hate her for what she'd done, she thought.

His eyes traveled down her to her bare feet. "There are some socks in the bottom drawer."

"Thank you." She quickly knelt and opened the drawer, fishing through the socks and sweaters. She saw a pair of thick athletic socks and reached for them, pushing aside a sweater.

Her hand stopped, and she almost smiled. It was a woman's sweater, a lavender pullover, the style she'd favored so long ago.

Then she saw the monogrammed *M* on the front. There was another sweater under that one and a set of panties and bra.

"What's wrong?" he asked.

Exhaustion, her cold and disappointment made her temper flare.

"Stop hovering over me," she snapped, standing with the socks in hand. "I don't need your help."

"No, I guess you've never needed anything from me," he retorted.

Rachel couldn't help looking at the open drawer again, and John followed her gaze.

Slowly he bent and picked up the sweater, then let it fall onto the underwear. "Is this what your mood is all about?" he asked, standing.

"I don't want to argue tonight," she said, regretting her outburst.

"I was married to the woman, Rachel," he said. "You're bound to find something of hers lying around. What difference does it make to you, anyway? I'm sure you have enough souvenirs from your former lover."

She nearly winced at his words, making John take a step toward her. "Of course," he said with quiet anger. "You have a permanent souvenir—your son."

"Don't," she said, turning away.

"Don't what?" he demanded. "What is it you want me not to do, Rachel? Do you even know what it is yourself?"

"Don't bring up the past," she whispered.

"You can't pretend it didn't happen, Rachel. Not when you came back here. And not while you're in this house."

The knowledge of how deeply she had hurt him made her want to cry. But she stood her ground instead, willing herself not to show her weakness.

"I shouldn't stay here," she said shakily. "I should go back to the cabin."

She made a tentative move toward the door, but John stepped in front of her, blocking her path. She raised her eyes to his and froze at the anger burning there. His eyes dropped lower, and she realized suddenly that she'd let the towel fall to the floor. He had a clear view of her breasts, visible through the thin fabric of the T-shirt.

"Go to bed, Rachel," he said sharply, his eyes rising to her face.

"John, I—"

"Go to bed, dammit!"

Before she could react he swung her up in his arms and carried her to the bed, depositing her on it without ceremony. But he didn't push himself away. He leaned over her, his mouth twisted, his eyes reflecting pain.

"Why did you have to come back here?" he demanded hoarsely. One hand began to caress her neck, making Rachel shiver as sexual awareness rippled through her.

"Why, Rachel?" he asked again, but this time his voice was softer. "Why torture both of us like this?"

She opened her mouth to tell him that she had never meant to cause either of them so much pain, but his mouth came down on hers, swallowing the words.

"Do you know how much I've thought about you, Rachel?" he whispered raggedly, raising his mouth for only a moment before kissing her again. His hand stroked down the front of her T-shirt and found her breast, urgently caressing it through the fabric until she thought she would drown in the sensations.

Rachel groaned and twisted beneath him, trying to press her body as closely to his as she could. All these years, and she still wanted him so much! So much that no other man had come close to touching her heart.

Rachel kissed him back without reserve, needing his touch and his kisses as balm for the ache inside her.

His mouth moved to her throat, and she arched, starved for his touch.

Eleven years ago she had thought that she would spare him unnecessary pain by telling a lie. Now she saw that she had only caused more pain.

"What have I done?" she murmured raggedly, remorse making her throat go dry.

John's head lifted from her throat, his eyes glistening with need. He looked dazed for a second, and then he seemed to recover himself.

"It was my fault," he said, quickly levering himself away from her. He stood with his back to her and lowered his head, his fingers pushing at his temple. "I'm sorry, Rachel," he said in a flat voice. "It won't happen again."

"John, wait," she said, but he was already halfway to the door. "Don't go."

He stopped and turned to look at her.

"If I'd said don't go eleven years ago, what would you have answered?" he asked.

Rachel flushed, knowing that John already knew the answer, and he condemned her for it.

"Good night, Rachel."

The door shut behind him, and she lay back on the pillow, her heart still pounding in her throat.

Don't go. She heard herself saying the words again, and then the tears finally came.

Five

Rachel awoke suddenly, disoriented, as someone opened the bedroom door. She had slept fitfully, dreaming of John and coming awake to find herself alone.

She could hear water running somewhere, making her wonder groggily why John had left the shower on.

But the man walking through the bedroom door wasn't John. It was George Edwards, humming and treading heavily.

"Sleeping kind of late this morning, aren't you, John?" he said, then stopped short and adjusted his glasses. "Oh, heavens, Rachel! I didn't expect… I mean, I didn't know… What I mean to say—"

"George, it's not what it looks like," Rachel groaned, but her words were all but unintelligible in the face of her morning hoarseness from the cold and George's continued babbling.

"Now, Rachel Tucker," George elaborated, ignoring her attempt at explanation. "This is none of my business, I know, but you and John have a history as such. The entire

town of Pierce knows that. And I don't want to see either of
you hurt again, inasmuch as I'm fond of the both of you."

"I only spent the night!" Rachel protested, but her voice
was still a croak. It was just as well George hadn't understood that, she thought, because it wasn't any better than
what George was surmising.

"How are you doing, George?" John asked lazily from
the bathroom doorway. Rachel took one look at him and
groaned again. She carefully kept her eyes above the large
bath towel wrapped around his waist. That only gave her a
view of his broad chest, droplets of water clinging to the
dark hair there. He was toweling his wet hair and ignoring
her.

"Damned if I know how I am," George said pointedly.
"It's you two I'm worried about."

John's eyes flickered to Rachel as if noticing her for the
first time.

"I told Rachel to spend the night here," he said casually.
"The roof leaks in the cabin bedroom, and I don't want the
ceiling falling down on her. She's going to have to stay here
until I can get to the repairs."

"I'm *not* moving in here," Rachel said indignantly, but
no one seemed to be paying any attention to her. She supposed it was difficult to take a woman caught sleeping in a
man's bed, wearing his T-shirt to boot, seriously. Remembering that the T-shirt afforded little real coverage, she
grabbed the covers and pulled them to her chin.

"I guess the cabin is in pretty bad shape," George said,
sitting on the end of the bed and scratching his chin
thoughtfully. "Should I bring in a contractor?"

John shook his head. "I can do the repairs, but I can't get
to them until this flood threat is over."

"Well, I suppose in the meantime Rachel can stay here,"
George said, still rubbing his chin. He glanced at Rachel,
who was about to object again when John spoke.

"You know, when Rachel's gone, you ought to think
about renting out the cabin."

"I'm not leaving," Rachel blurted out.

This time both men turned to stare at her. "What did you say?" John demanded, frowning.

"I said I'm staying here—in Pierce," she said with less conviction in the face of their incredulous expressions. "What's wrong?" she demanded. "Nobody passed a new law outlawing returnees, did they?"

George smiled and reached over to pat her leg. "No, they didn't, honey, and I'll be the first to welcome you. But are you sure this is what you want?"

"Yes," she said testily, tired suddenly of everyone else's expectations where her life was concerned. "Very much."

"We're always looking for tellers at the bank," George said, "but I don't know that it would offer you much of a challenge."

"I was planning on opening an investment service," Rachel said carefully. "With all the farmers and small-business owners around here, I think I'd have plenty of business."

"Well, you probably would at that," George said, brightening.

"Not that my opinion counts for much," John said dryly, "but how long do you think it will be before you're homesick for the city again?"

George waved away John's objection. "Your opinion isn't worth beans in this," George said, winking at Rachel.

"One other thing," Rachel said hesitantly. "I'd like to buy the cabin, George. That is, if you think you'd be willing to sell."

"The cabin? But, Rachel, honey, it's not fit to live in."

"It would be—after the repairs are made." Seeing the skepticism creeping back into their faces, she went on earnestly. "It's such a good place for a young boy to grow up. David would have room to play and a place to bring his friends."

"Ah, David's the key here, is he?" George said, softening. "Well, you're right, Rachel. It's a good place to raise a child. I'd be happy to sell you the cabin."

"Really?" Rachel beamed, her smile wavering when she turned and met the distrust in John's eyes.

"Though I've never negotiated a real-estate deal in quite this kind of setting," George said, adjusting his glasses again and grinning. "You come on by and see me when you have time, and we'll work out the terms."

George stood, still shaking his head and chuckling. He stopped in the doorway and turned. "Darned if I didn't forget to tell you why I came over. You remember Myron Taylor up in Cedarwood?" When John nodded, George said, "He does his banking with me. Fine man. His oldest daughter is getting married this summer."

"And you've come to extend a wedding invitation?" John asked dryly. "A man could turn to stone in this towel waiting for you to come to the point, George."

"All right, all right." George grinned. "Myron couldn't get all of his feeder pigs out when the levee broke last night. He's got four left that are up on the roof of the confinement building. Think you could run up there with your boat?"

"Sure. Soon as I get some breakfast. Where does he want me to take them?"

"He'll meet you where Landers Road runs into the river. The ground's still firm enough there for him to park his pickup. I'll call him as soon as I get home."

"Tell him I'll leave here in about half an hour."

Rachel threw back the covers and stood as soon as she heard the front door close behind George.

"And where are you going?" John demanded.

"With you," she said without hesitation.

"You belong in bed," he told her, scowling.

"I'm feeling much better, and I'm not about to lie in bed all day," she protested.

"Then do something in the kitchen," he said dismissively, turning for the door.

"The kitchen!" Rachel repeated in stunned irritation. "You've turned into the biggest, most pigheaded chauvinist in Pierce, John David McClennon!" She threw a pillow at him, hitting him in the back of the head.

John turned around slowly as Rachel waited, suddenly wondering if throwing a pillow at him had been such a good idea. There was just the hint of a smile in his eyes as he picked up the pillow and walked toward her. Rachel stood her ground, her breath caught in her throat.

He stopped in front of her, his eyes traveling down the front of her borrowed T-shirt.

"No, you never belonged in the kitchen, did you, Rachel?" His voice was teasing, and it made her heart thud against her ribs. Oh, Lord, she thought miserably. With one look he could still make her as breathless as a giddy schoolgirl. But she would get over it. She had no other choice.

John tossed the pillow onto the bed, his eyes never leaving her face. His hand moved to his waist, and she watched in disbelief as he tugged at the towel around his hips. He laughed as she quickly closed her eyes.

"If you're going with me, wear something you can get dirty," he said, and she realized his voice was coming from the doorway now.

She opened one eye in time to see the back of his blue boxer shorts as he vanished into the hall.

He'd been teasing her!

It was an incredible revelation, because it was the last thing she'd expected from John. Maybe they could get along, after all.

Rachel could feel John's eyes on her as he drove toward Cedarwood in the pickup. She stared resolutely out the window, not wanting to provoke him out of the decent mood he was in for once.

He hadn't said anything to her when she came downstairs in an old pair of his jeans, belted at the waist and rolled at the ankles, and one of his blue plaid flannel shirts. He'd taken a long, hard look at her, then used a pair of scissors to shorten the pants.

Rachel had made toast while John fried eggs, and they ate in silence. The radio was on, and John listened intently to the weather forecast, a possibility of more rain. She could see that his mind was still on the levee.

Before they left, he got her an old pair of knee-high boots and stuffed rags in the ends until they fit her feet snugly.

The air bore a chill this morning, but the sun more than made up for it. Rachel could feel a pleasant drowsiness coming over her as the warmth bathed her face through the truck window.

John turned the truck onto what Rachel remembered was Landers Road. He drove around a Road Closed sign, slowing as the truck encountered ruts and mud. "Myron'll see the truck and wait here," he said as she turned questioning eyes on him. "Now I need your help."

"Me?" she said doubtfully.

"I'm going to turn the truck around and back toward the water. When I get close, I want you to take over while I walk beside the boat. I need to see how deep the water is."

"Back toward the water?" she repeated, again doubtfully. She didn't see any water, and she knew they were a half mile from the river.

"You'll see," he said grimly.

She did see a few minutes later as he backed the truck and attached trailer around a bend in the road. What looked like a huge lake came into view. But she knew there was no lake here. This was the river's overflow, as big and murky as the river itself.

John stopped the truck and hopped out. "Scoot over and start backing slowly," he ordered as he disappeared around the back of the truck. "I'll tell you when to stop."

Rachel slid to the driver's side, adjusted the seat forward and took a deep breath. "John David McClennon, I'll get you for this," she muttered. He had done this to her countless times when they were both children, simply gave her instructions for something she'd never done before, then left her on her own. She supposed that in a way he had given her the confidence she'd lacked as a small child. She had always figured that if John thought she could do it, then she would darn well do it. She couldn't let him down.

"You do remember how to back up a stick shift, don't you?" he asked, appearing again at the window. "You know, the big *R* on the shift column."

"Silly me," she muttered in his direction. "Here I was looking for a *BU,* for back up."

She thought she heard him laugh as he disappeared around the back again. She looked in the rearview mirror and saw him to the side, walking beside the small motorboat on the trailer. He picked up a large stick from the boat and hollered for her to start backing.

"Well, here goes nothing." She sighed, pushing in the clutch and forcing the gearshift into reverse. A loud grinding noise ensued, but thankfully John didn't comment.

She slowly backed up the truck, her eyes glued to the mirror, her heart hammering. She could see John periodically thrust the stick into the water, measuring the depth.

"Whoa!" he hollered. "Right here."

She turned off the engine and set the brake before climbing out. Her feet landed in about eighteen inches of water, but John's old boots kept her dry.

He loaded a small wire kennel like the kind used to transport dogs, and she supposed it was to hold the pigs.

John unhooked the boat from the trailer and pushed it into the water. He had her get in and don a life jacket before he pushed the boat farther into the floodwaters, then climbed in facing her.

In short time he had the engine started, and they were drifting slowly down what used to be a road.

John kept his eyes trained on the watery landscape ahead. He had driven this road in a car countless times, and now he forced himself to recall every fence, every mailbox. If he caught the boat motor on even one post he'd forgotten, he and Rachel could be stranded out here.

Rachel was home to stay. The words had repeated themselves in his head like a litany all morning until he thought his brain would explode. He had wanted nothing more than for Rachel to pack up and head back to the city as soon as possible, which was why his mellow mood was all the more inexplicable to him. He had meant to keep a brick wall between Rachel and his emotions, but he couldn't control how she made him feel.

Her staying here would present all kinds of unwanted complications, but still he couldn't make himself be angry with her.

There had been such a longing in her eyes when she'd said she was staying here. He doubted it was longing for him, but it was certainly for something from the past.

Maybe there would be a denouement of sorts, a peace for both of them, with Rachel's homecoming. The pain he'd felt at her leaving was too much to leave unresolved.

John recognized the top of the flag on Myron's mailbox sticking out of the water off to his right, and he slowed the boat. Even the dedicated rural mail carriers would be hard-pressed to deliver anything other than fish here, he thought grimly.

He glanced at Rachel, her head to the side as she took in the devastation over her shoulder, and saw tears in the corners of her eyes.

"Hey," he said gently.

"It's awful," she said without turning around, her voice strained. "Did you see that armchair float by?"

"What's done is done," he said.

It was how she supposed farmers survived, by not agonizing over the things they couldn't control. And there was so much they couldn't control.

Rachel had always railed against the fates she couldn't subdue, but John would just laugh. "There's nothing you can do about it," he'd tell her, and she'd end up punching his arm.

John looked away from her and gritted his teeth. The water made him angry, too, but he'd never been one to fling himself against the wind the way Rachel did. He supposed he should have done that years ago when Rachel left him, followed her halfway across the country if he had to and made her see what she was throwing away. But he hadn't.

He'd hardened the shell around himself, instead, and now it was too late.

He made himself concentrate on maneuvering the boat, throttling back the motor almost completely. He remembered where the fence ended, and if he turned right there, he could make the farrowing house without incident.

The squeal of pigs greeted him as the boat pulled alongside the roof of the metal building. It was beginning to buckle at the bottom from the weight of the water, and he gently bumped the boat as close as he could.

"All right, city girl," he told Rachel. "How good are you at catching pigs?"

"The best," she assured him, standing precariously in the boat and holding the roof for balance.

Hungry and frightened, the pigs scampered just out of reach. Rachel managed to snag one's leg, and she held tight as the small pig squealed in protest. She let go of the roof long enough to grasp the pig under its belly with her other hand, and then she was lifting it into the boat. John opened the wire carrier and helped her secure the pig inside.

John climbed onto the roof after the remaining three pigs scrambled out of their reach. He caught the pigs one by one and handed them to Rachel, who slipped them into the pen.

Everything was going well until the final pig panicked and ran down the length of the roof, squealing.

John slid onto his face, catching the pig's back leg just before he would have plunged into the water. Cursing under his breath and occasionally out loud, John dragged the pig backward until he could grip it with both hands. "Get in the boat, you stupid, beady-eyed, snouted slab of bacon!" he growled, nearly tossing the pig to Rachel.

She bent down to put the pig in the pen with the others, ducking her head so John wouldn't see how close she was to laughter.

"What?" he demanded when she straightened, her lips twitching. She half crouched when the boat rocked.

"Nothing," she said, but then her composure crumbled, and she burst out laughing.

"What?" he repeated with more irritation. He had risen to his knees on the roof and towered over her, glowering, his hands on his hips.

"I don't know who was more aggravated with this whole deal," she said, trying not to laugh. "You or the pig."

"He was pretty put out about it, wasn't he?" John said after a pause. His face softened. "And pretty ungrateful for someone who was just rescued from a roof."

"Definitely," Rachel agreed.

"About as ungrateful as you were when I helped you win the greased-pig contest when you were in third grade," he said.

"I won that contest all on my own!" she protested, standing to her full height and not caring if the boat tipped or not.

"If you recall, I'm the one who lured that pig into a corner by holding my cotton candy through the fence rail. You were so busy falling on your face in the mud, you couldn't even grab his tail."

"John David McClennon! I resent that! I outran three older boys to get to that pig first, and that pig had no more interest in your cotton candy than he had in you! I won that contest all on my own."

They stared at each other, heads cocked to the side, hands on hips in argumentative style. Then John began to smile. He threw back his head and laughed, his deep voice echoing across the water and the deserted farm.

"You're still touchy about that greased-pig contest, Rachel!"

He was laughing when she reached out, grabbed his arm and tugged hard. With a grunt of surprise, John came tumbling toward her. Rachel hadn't really planned beyond that point, and they both nearly ended up in the water as the boat pitched back and forth. John's knee hit Rachel's hip, knocking her backward to the seat. He was sprawled almost on top of her, and Rachel lay pinned with her legs dangling over the edge of the boat. The pigs squealed loudly from their pen.

The hard pressure of John's body on top of hers left Rachel breathless. She nearly groaned aloud. Actually, she might have, because John shifted as soon as he recovered his balance.

"Are you crazy, Rachel?" he demanded, only half-angry. "You could have dumped you, me and the pigs in that water."

"It was worth it," she assured him, reaching around to rub her lower back where it had hit the seat. "You looked so smug."

"Are you hurt?" he asked with sudden concern, levering himself down to the seat beside her. He lifted her—actually *his*—shirt in the back and probed lightly with his fingers. Rachel suppressed a sigh. "You scraped yourself," he said, his fingers gently rubbing. "You'll have a bruise."

Rachel let her eyes drift closed, thinking of nothing at the moment but John's strong, warm fingers and how good they felt on her back.

If she concentrated only on the sensations running riot through her body, she could pretend that this was eleven years ago and she and John were still in love. She could pretend that he still cared what happened to her.

"Why did you leave me, Rachel?" John asked abruptly, the question coming out of left field, as it were, although any left field near at hand was under water.

Rachel's eyes snapped open. She turned to see his face, registered the pain and quickly looked away.

"I was young, John. I...wanted different things."

"Different than what you want now?"

She hesitated. It was so hard to maintain the lie, to make him believe that she had stopped loving him then, that she was someone she wasn't.

"Life is filled with circles, isn't it?" she said instead. "No matter where we start, we often end up back at the beginning."

"It won't work," he said relentlessly. "Neither of us can go back to the beginning."

"No," she agreed quietly.

The pigs squealed in protest again. John removed his fingers from Rachel's back and moved to the boat's motor.

"We'd better get our cargo delivered," he said, refusing to meet her eyes when she sought his.

She knew that he was still angry inside, but he sounded resigned. She'd given such a load of pain when she'd left. And she'd never meant to hurt him.

She remembered how her mother used to sing an old song, and the lyrics echoed in Rachel's head in cadence with the boat's motor. *You always hurt the one you love.*

She had never stopped loving him, not even when she was pregnant with his child and he married someone else. Hurting him, she had hurt herself as well. That love had never gone away, and just seeing John again made her heart swell with remembered pain.

Rachel leaned over as she began to cough. She could feel him looking at her now, but she kept her face carefully away from his eyes. John had always read her expressions too easily. That was why she'd lied to him on the phone about another man. Seeing her face, he would have guessed the truth.

Sighing, she stole a look at him. He was almost quick enough to look away from her before she saw him. But not quite.

Strangers. Strangers with a past. That's what she and John were. But it wouldn't do any good to think about that now. At the moment they had pigs to deliver.

Myron Taylor was waiting for them at Landers Road, parked next to John's pickup. John pulled the boat close, then waded out into the water, handing the pigs one by one to the farmer.

"Going to rain again," Myron observed laconically. "Weather station says just a drizzle. Shouldn't raise the river."

"Hope not," John agreed.

Myron thanked them, tipped his hat and drove off with his pigs. Rachel was expecting John to push the boat to its trailer, but he climbed back in instead and turned the boat back toward the deeper water.

Rachel didn't speak as they rode on, not wanting to break the tenuous peace between them. Despite John's sudden question about her leaving, he didn't seem resentful. The teasing about the greased-pig contest had gone a long way to easing the pain between them.

She couldn't have imagined this a year ago, Rachel thought in wonder as she looked around. Here she was, traveling a surreal landscape with John McClennon beside her. She couldn't decide which was more alien, the flood or John's quiet presence.

The sky was darkening, and the wind freshened.

"Over there," John said, pointing.

She followed his finger and saw a fawn's head above the water. The animal was bobbing, struggling to swim but disoriented.

John guided the boat slowly toward the animal, and when they were beside it, he reached over and hauled it into the boat. "Hold its legs," he ordered Rachel, clasping them together until she could get a grip.

The fawn cried with short, helpless bleats, breathing hard between its struggles. Rachel held its legs tightly, talking to it in a soothing voice.

John guided the boat toward a clump of bushes that rose from the water like eerie green mushrooms. He stopped the motor and let the boat drift until it bumped land. Stepping out into water up to his knees, he took the fawn from Rachel and walked to higher ground. He set it down where the ground was dry and backed away.

The fawn tried to run, but shaking limbs wouldn't carry it far. It stumbled and stopped, then gathered strength and ran off.

"The ground's dry from here on out," John said, turning back to Rachel. He looked around, scanning the hill rising before them. "Do you know where we are?"

Rachel shook her head. It was all too unfamiliar with the water covering so much.

"Jake's old fishing cabin is just over the hill. Remember?"

Yes, she remembered, and it made her flush. His voice was noncommittal, and she couldn't read his expression.

She and John had made love here one hot summer day when she was home from college. They had gone fishing to get some time alone to talk, but as usually happened with them, the talk turned into something else.

"I should check on it for him," John said. "Coming?"

Rachel hesitated, then nodded. She was about to climb out of the boat when John stepped closer and picked her up in his arms.

Seeing her startled expression, he laughed. "The water comes over your boot tops here," he said. "And you haven't had a tetanus shot, have you?"

Rachel shook her head, still clinging to his neck when he set her down. She remembered at last to let go and flushed again.

"We'll have to remedy that if you're going to keep sandbagging," he said. "Here, hold this while I pull the boat in."

She caught the rope and waited until he'd pulled the boat up high enough. Taking the rope from her suddenly numb fingers, he tied it to a sturdy bush.

"Come on," he said gruffly, making Rachel sigh. One touch and he was back to the old anger again.

Rachel was behind him as they walked up the hill, and it took all of John's willpower not to turn around and look at her. Carrying her from the boat had sapped what little resistance he had left.

The intervening years had done nothing to diminish the feelings she aroused in him. The slightest touch—his finger against her skin, her hair on his flesh—and he had to fight a fierce urge to make love to her.

He'd been rejected once by her, and he wouldn't chance it again, not even in a fleeting encounter. What had gone before was over.

Rachel was breathing hard when they reached the top of the hill, and she slowed down as raspy coughs shook her.

John had stopped to give her time to catch up, though he might be oblivious to her existence for all the attention he paid to her. Rachel felt shaky and off guard. John did that to her. She never knew what he was thinking now. In the past she would only have had to read his face.

"A little the worse for wear," he said, and she looked past him at the cabin in the clearing. Some shingles had long since blown off the roof, and the windows were dirty and cracked. But, all in all, it looked much the same as it had years ago. It was a small A-frame built of split logs. The front door opened onto a compact porch, where a small pile of old firewood still lay.

Rain was beginning to fall in a light mist, and John looked to the sky. He seemed to be thinking out loud when he spoke. "The forecast said scattered light showers," he said. "Our sandbags were two feet over flood level last night, so the levee should be okay." He swung his eyes to Rachel. "I'd better get you somewhere dry before that cold of yours turns into pneumonia."

"I like standing in the rain," she said, tilting her head up to let it bathe her face.

"One of these days I'm going to make you do what I tell you to do," he warned.

"The river doesn't stand a chance against you," she said, teasing him. "John David McClennon against the forces of nature."

"I wish it were that easy," he said, giving a smile that didn't reach his eyes. "After crop failures, drought and flood, I don't feel so omnipotent."

"You act it," she assured him, only half jesting.

"There's one force of nature I've had no luck controlling," he said with a gleam in his eye. "And that's you, Rachel Tucker. I tell you to go rest, and you work harder than ever. I tell you to get in out of the rain, and you stand out in it just to be obstinate. Maybe if you got really wet, you'd listen to me."

He began advancing on her, and Rachel backed away. She saw him eyeing a bucket beside the porch. It was dented, but apparently intact, since it was full of rainwater collected over the last several days. John's eyes followed hers, and he grinned.

"Now, John," she said, trying to placate him. "You don't want me to get pneumonia, do you?"

"Oh, I'll dry you off," he assured her, his grin widening.

He reached for Rachel, and she danced away with a shriek, then ran for the cabin.

John caught up with her as she reached the porch, his hands closing over her arms and turning her to him. They were both laughing, laughter that slowly died as their eyes locked. She took a step backward and found her back against the cabin wall. She could hear the rain lightly dripping from the porch eaves, a sound that was a gentle counterpoint to her own ragged heartbeat.

Rachel lifted her mouth to his, unable to even pretend that she didn't want his kiss. Without preamble, his hands released her to encircle her waist and pull her against him. His mouth took hers with a hunger that left her breathless. The kiss was electric in its effect, singeing her nerve endings into acute awareness of the man holding her.

He lifted his mouth briefly, then took hers again with the same deliberation and need.

The kiss went on forever, years of need invested in it. Rachel clutched the back of John's neck, afraid she might fall if she didn't hold on. *Time was supposed to heal wounds,* she thought crazily, her mouth hungrily responding to John's. But there was still a gaping wound inside her heart, a wound that hurt even now with John pressed against her.

When he raised his head to look at her, his blue eyes were the darkness of an approaching thunderstorm. He let her look at his face, and he made no attempt to hide the obvious pain there.

"We have to go back to the boat," he said harshly.

Rachel glanced past him at the sky. "The rain?"

He shook his head impatiently as if he hadn't expected her to be so dense. "Don't you know what you're doing to me?" he ground out, his hands tightening on her waist. "If

we don't leave now, Rachel, I don't think I could stop myself from . . . taking you."

Rachel's breath caught in her throat. Time hung between
them so heavily that it might have been a second or a year
before she answered. "I don't want you to stop." Her voice
didn't sound like her own, but she didn't feel like herself
right now. All that mattered was the feel of John Mc-
Clennon's body loving her.

Wanting her, she amended. Though she had never quite
stopped loving him, he had certainly thrown her out of his
heart. But at the moment her body didn't care. She needed
John so much that she was nearly whimpering as he held her
to his side and forced the cabin door open.

"I owe Jake a new lock," he said, but the heat in his eyes
said that Jake and the lock were the last things on his mind
now.

Rachel saw the hesitation cloud his eyes, and she stiff-
ened. "Rachel," he said quietly, "are you on the pill?"

She shook her head.

"I don't have any condoms with me," he said bluntly.
John had always spoken his mind with her, and she was
grateful for it now.

"It's all right," she said. "It's the wrong time of the
month."

He looked at her a moment longer, then surprised her by
sweeping her up in his arms, trying to smile but not quite
succeeding. There had always been teasing and laughter
along with the passion between them, but today was different. This was too urgent, too emotional for laughter. This
was as necessary as breath itself.

"Kiss me," he commanded her, holding his mouth to hers
as he carried her to the bed in the alcove of the one-room
cabin. He started to set her on the bare mattress, then
thought better of it when he realized how musty it was.
"Wait," he said, putting her on her feet and pressing his
fingers to her lips as if afraid she might not wait after all, but
bolt out the door instead. "Wait, I'll be right back."

He couldn't even think straight, he thought in desperation. He needed her so much that he was making a fool of himself over simple housekeeping matters.

John found a clean blanket in a chest by the wall and hurried back to Rachel with it. He pulled her close again and kissed her as though incredulous that she was still there. After spreading the blanket on the bed, he picked her up again and gently laid her down, then pulled off her boots and socks.

"Is it comfortable enough?" he asked. She was a city woman, accustomed to apartment beds with sheets and blankets that were washed more than once every few months.

"It doesn't matter," she said. "I want you."

His heart swelled then, and he went to her, kneeling beside the bed and tracing her lips with his finger.

She rolled to her side, facing him, her hand reaching out to explore him, as well. She curled her fingers in his thick hair, the strands coarse and black as midnight against her pale skin. Drawing his face toward her, she kissed him, then groaned and planted small kisses all over his jaw.

His skin was slightly beard roughened, sensitizing her lips and making her ache to feel all of him against her, inside her.

Impatient, she sat up and tugged at his red T-shirt, trying to pull it up over his chest. She murmured in approval as she skimmed the firm, bare skin, his thick, dark chest hair tickling her palms. For so long she had touched a man like this only in her dreams, and even then the only man who invaded her sleep was John. Now she sought respite from her rising tide of desire by feeding all her senses.

Pulling him to her, Rachel laid her head against his chest and breathed in the musky scent of his skin. She could hear his heart hammering beneath her ear, and it drove her to bolder explorations.

Her hand slipped beneath the waistband of his jeans, and she stroked his flat stomach and the wiry hair below.

John groaned her name. He stood then, giving her a half-apologetic, wry look as he adjusted his jeans.

Then he was shedding his clothes.

Rachel watched him with unabashed pleasure, reaching out to graze his naked thighs when he stepped from his pants. Hard, physical work had honed his muscles into sharp planes, giving his frame a spare, powerful look. It was evident that she aroused him, and he was making no effort to hide it. They had always been comfortable with each other's bodies. Time hadn't stolen that.

John sat on the edge of the bed and drew Rachel up until he had her pressed against him. She shivered with need and ran a trembling hand down his back.

She could feel his breath warm and quick against her neck as he held her. Then his hands slipped to the front of her borrowed flannel shirt, and he began undoing buttons with shaking fingers.

John took a long, probing look into her eyes before he slid the shirt from her shoulders, and she shrugged out of it.

It landed on the floor as his fingers began a slow, tantalizing exploration of her flimsy bra. His touch through the silky fabric was electric, making her body hum with sensual awareness.

He unhooked the bra and let it fall to the floor.

"Say my name," he said softly as his fingers played lightly over her nipples, arousing them to hard peaks.

His name was a quivering whisper on her lips.

John's mouth took hers again. At the same time his hands undid her belt and began to tug down the jeans. When they reached her hips, he levered her toward him and pulled them off.

She found herself sitting on his lap, naked after he'd disposed of her panties, her head on his shoulder and her arms curled around his neck. His breath was a teasing caress on her cheek.

"Now," he said when they were both completely undressed, "look at me, Rachel. I want to see you. Maybe then I'll stop seeing you in my head every night."

The admission had been wrenched from him, making her ache for both of them. There were years of memories between them, imagined and real.

"Don't," she whispered, pressing her fingers to his lips, not wanting to think about the past.

He caught her fingers in his hand and brought them to his bare chest. Swiftly his mouth moved to hers, taking her before she could even think. This kiss was different. The others had spoken of longing, lost chances, desire. This one claimed her. She was John David McClennon's woman, for this hour if no more, and he meant her to know it.

Rachel clung to him, matching his kiss in intensity and raw emotion.

"John," she groaned. "John, love me."

"Not yet," he whispered raggedly, soothing her with gentle caresses. "I don't want this fast, Rachel. It's the memory that will stay with me the rest of my life, and I mean it to last a long time."

He suckled her breasts, his fingers teasing and tracing a path around her nipple while his mouth gave her such pleasure that she thought she would faint. Her head fell backward, and she groaned.

John caught her to him again and lowered her to the bed. He knelt over her, his eyes alight with a fierce need that made her stomach clench in response.

His hands, work roughened but gentle, stroked along her thighs, making her writhe beneath him as they caressed the softness between her legs.

Unable to stay still, she raised herself enough to touch his legs, as well, and the hard proof of his desire. He groaned, and Rachel flicked at his flat brown nipples with her tongue.

"Now," she urged him, her kisses trailing lower until his body jerked in response. "I need you now."

"Yes, now," he said on a hoarse note as he slid his body over hers.

Rachel arched against him in compelling excitement as he entered her slowly. She murmured his name over and over as her hands clutched his back, urging him to satisfy her hunger.

"John, please," she groaned when he slowly withdrew and just as slowly pushed in again. Her hips thrust against him.

His breathing was ragged. His eyes as they held hers were dark sapphires. "Tell me you need me, Rachel," he whispered hoarsely.

"Make love to me, John," she said. "I need you to make love to me."

He shook his head, poised inside her without moving. "Tell me you need me, Rachel. *Me.*"

She twisted beneath him, her eyes glittering with passion as she met his demanding gaze. "Yes," she murmured. She loved him, but that wasn't what he wanted to hear. "I need you, John."

He pushed into her sharply then, his breath expelling on a groan. "Tell me again, sweetheart," he asked her, his rhythm bringing her excruciating pleasure.

She told him, whispering the words, finally crying out his name when the incredible sensations drove her to release.

Six

Rachel was dreaming about her son. Specifically about John and her son. She had to pick up David at the St. Louis airport today, and she was dreaming that she was late.

In the way that nonsense seems perfectly normal in dreams, John was racing her to the airport. She couldn't find David, and then she saw that John had reached him first. John was telling David something, and David was shaking his head. Then David began to cry, and John walked away. He passed Rachel, a triumphant smile on his face.

Rachel came awake abruptly, her hands and face damp with perspiration. She was lying on a blanket, half of it thrown over her naked body. She moved slightly, not sure where she was, and she felt the residual soreness between her legs.

John had made love to her.

Discovering that she was alone in the bed, she looked around the room. She hadn't paid much attention to it when John had carried her in.

Patches of dim light filtered in through the bare, dirty windows. She couldn't hear any more water dripping from the eaves, so the rain must have stopped. Ragged and dusty rugs were scattered on the wood floor. A small kitchen table sat in front of one window, its top littered with soda cans and magazines. Judging from the thickness of the dust, the place had been deserted a long time.

Rachel could hear John moving about in the small bathroom off the kitchen. A moment later he came out. Not realizing that she was awake, he padded across the floor in his jeans and socks and stopped at the window, his back to her. Resting one forearm on the frame, he stared out.

She couldn't see his face, but the set of his shoulders conveyed a weariness.

She should tell him about David. The man had the right to know that he had a son. She possessed enough self-awareness to realize that her dream was her subconscious way of nudging her into action. But it was also an expression of her fear that John would reject his son. Not because he didn't want his son, but because of what Rachel had done to him.

That would devastate David, to find a father and then lose him. It would devastate her, as well.

She had agonized so often over telling John about David. If she had thought that the knowledge would have brought John some measure of peace, she wouldn't have hesitated. But in all likelihood it would have cost him his marriage, and what joy his son gave him would have been too tempered by the constraints of time and distance. She was too far away for John to see David often, and that would have chafed a proud man like John.

Rachel shivered slightly and shifted on the bed. Hearing her, John turned from the window.

Lying naked on the bed made her feel far too vulnerable to him, and she moved into a sitting position, dragging the blanket around her. She took a deep breath, wanting to tell him about David. They would meet for the first time in a few hours.

This is your son.

Rachel couldn't see John's expression with the light behind him, and his silence unnerved her. "So much for four-star hotels," she said lightly as she began shrugging into her clothes. "I guess we can't get any room service."

"I'm sorry it's not what you're used to," John said, a harsh edge to his voice, making Rachel immediately regret her teasing.

"John, I didn't mean—"

"You'll be back with laundered sheets and maid service soon enough," he said, pushing away from the window. "I guarantee you won't stay here long, despite your wide-eyed protests that you want to settle down in Pierce. You were eager enough to leave this town one time before—and me with it."

"It seems I made the right choice," she shot back in anger. He was being deliberately cruel. All of her feelings of tenderness fled as John strode to the door, then slammed it shut behind him. Rachel cursed under her breath and finished dressing as quickly as she could.

They had never resolved anything with their lovemaking, she remembered. It had only uncovered emotions that were better left unearthed.

It was a silent, tense ride back in the boat, interrupted only by Rachel's occasional cough. When they reached the truck, John gave Rachel terse instructions on backing the truck. He loaded the boat onto the trailer and climbed back in the driver's seat, barely waiting for her to scoot to her own side.

Rachel bit off an irritated expletive and stared out the window. Tears came to her eyes, angry, bitter tears. He'd made her tell him how much she needed him before he made love to her, and now he shut her out. She supposed it was payback time. He was going to show her that he could walk away from her as easily as she had walked away from him. Only it hadn't been easy for her. It had been the hardest thing she'd ever done.

George's car was back in the drive when they pulled in at John's house, and George sat on the top porch step, slowly rolling a cigarette paper.

"I don't smoke anymore," he told them when they got out, "but it's good exercise for my fingers. So, you get those pigs rounded up?"

John nodded shortly and began unhitching the trailer.

Rachel stood on the bottom step, watching him and thinking how miserable she was.

Deciding that her misery wasn't going to improve around John, she turned to George and said, "I guess I'll hit the road for St. Louis. I want to get there early."

"St. Louis? What are you going there for?" George asked without any pretense of tact.

"I'm picking up my son at the airport."

"Oh, yeah. But, Rachel, you're going to have to drive way out of your way to get there. The bridge closed after last night's levee break, remember?"

No, she didn't remember. She supposed she'd been too addle brained over John McClennon to think about the bridge. Now what was she going to do?

"Let me drive you," George said.

"I'll take her," John's voice interrupted, and Rachel turned to find herself staring into emotionless blue eyes. He was wiping his hands on a rag, his forearms cording with the effort.

"Nonsense," Rachel said, not relishing the thought of sharing a car with John for a long trip. "Draw me a map of the shortest route, and I'll drive it myself."

John's jaw tightened. "You'll waste two hours going north to cross the bridge there and another two hours coming down the other side of the river, not to mention the remainder of the drive to St. Louis. It would be eight hours round trip, at the minimum."

Rachel was suddenly crestfallen. "But I'll never get to the airport on time," she said in dismay.

"Yes, you will," John said. "I'll fly you."

"You have a plane?" she asked skeptically.

"I have a pilot's license," John said shortly.

"He used to fly company planes for the compressor plant," George said. Rachel remembered that the plant was headquartered about twenty miles from here. "The president is a good friend. I'm sure he'll let John rent one of his private planes. It's a great idea." George stood as if everything was suddenly decided. "I've got to get going," he said. "I only came by to see if you and Rachel can come over for dinner tomorrow night."

"Can't make it," John said shortly. "But I'm sure Rachel can."

George looked from one to the other in amusement. "Well, I guess I don't need to have you throw me off the porch, John, before I get the idea. You and Rachel always did fight like cats and dogs. I must say I've missed that over the years." He chuckled and ambled down the steps. "I'll be leaving now. If either one or both of you want to come to dinner tomorrow, it'll be fine. Be interesting, too."

When George's car had pulled away, John glared at Rachel. "Go home and change," he said. "I'll pick you up as soon as I make a couple of phone calls."

"John, you don't have to do this," she said calmly, trying to be conciliatory and get him out of this obligation.

"Rachel, if I don't, your son is going to be standing by himself for a long time in the St. Louis airport, wondering what became of his mother."

The prospect of David waiting alone for her was argument enough. As a child, she'd waited alone for her mother so many times after school, and so many of those times her mother hadn't shown up.

"All right. Thank you." She walked away toward the bluff leading to the cabin, her back ramrod straight. George had been right. She and John had always fought like cats and dogs. But it had been a healthy kind of fighting between two strong people. What was going on between them now was more like a war.

John watched her walk away for a long time before he turned back to the house. She was struggling up the hill as if she was still tired. And she was coughing again. He didn't like the sound of her cough, but he wasn't going to say anything. There was no point in trying to tell Rachel Tucker what to do.

He phoned to reserve the plane, getting a friendly, cooperative response, as he always had. Sometimes he used the company planes to ferry sick children to distant hospitals when their families needed fast transportation and couldn't afford it. A local nurse volunteered to ride along and monitor the children. This wasn't an emergency of the same caliber, but in the eyes of the company it qualified.

He couldn't stop thinking of Rachel as he washed his face and changed clothes. Their lovemaking had been as intense and hungry as years ago, but he still wasn't sated with her. The more he touched Rachel, the more he wanted.

Which explained, but didn't excuse, his anger and abruptness with her at the cabin. But, dammit, he knew Rachel. She could leave here tomorrow without a backward glance. She was fickle and unpredictable, and she'd once left him for a man with more to offer. He had to admit that perhaps he was unconsciously trying to inflict some of the same pain on her that he'd felt when she left.

It wasn't a noble thought, and it did nothing to assuage the burning hunger inside his body.

John didn't get out of the truck when he pulled up in front of Rachel's cabin half an hour later. When she came out, she avoided his eyes, though he couldn't stop himself from looking her over.

She wore khaki pants, a pale green print blouse topped with a soft white cashmere sweater and low heels. She had brushed her hair and applied some light makeup. John couldn't seem to stop looking at her.

His irritation with himself made his voice gruffer than usual. "Do you think you can climb into a plane in those shoes?"

Rachel looked at him in surprise. "They're not very high. I usually get around quite well in them."

He grunted and pulled away, and she turned to look out the window. She was forever doing the wrong thing around John. She thought he couldn't possibly have an objection to the classic, understated clothes she was wearing. They were casual enough for travel but dressy enough to let David know that he was definitely worth dressing up for.

She probably should have worn jeans like John did. She couldn't help stealing a sideways glance at his thighs and remembering how they had felt molded to her when they made love. He had rolled up the sleeves of his blue chambray shirt. Her eyes moved over the light covering of hair on his forearms and slid on to his hands and long, firm fingers. Those fingers could be so arousing when they played over her body. But when he was in his current mood, the harshness of his voice could negate the gentleness of his hard body.

Rachel resolutely turned her eyes back to the window and stared out the rest of the trip to the small regional airport. John hopped out without looking at her and, over his shoulder, told her to wait for him.

It was almost half an hour before he returned, and she'd grown restless with anxiety. She wasn't a nervous flyer, but the smallest plane she'd ever ridden in was a commuter plane that seated twenty. She had a feeling that John's plane would be diminutive by comparison. And she wasn't crazy about small, confined places. In fact, she was almost phobic about them.

She was right.

When John finally returned and led her toward the tarmac, she saw two planes parked side by side.

Let it be the bigger one, she prayed earnestly.

Her heart sank when John turned toward the smaller plane, a single prop that looked to seat no more than two people. She was tempted to suggest that John leave her here while he picked up David, but she squared her shoulders for her son's sake and kept pace.

"The other one's in line for some maintenance," he told her as if reading her thoughts. He opened the door and stood on a small projection to show her where to put her foot. It was a tall step up, but with John's firm hand on her arm she made it. She settled into the seat next to the pilot's, her heart pounding.

She glanced over when John got in and realized that there were two more seats in the back. Still, she felt like a bug trapped in a very tiny glass jar.

Rachel found herself scanning the dials and gauges in front of her with no idea what any of them indicated. She pulled the seat belt across her chest, fumbling with it until John took the metal piece from her numb fingers and snapped it in place.

Rachel kept her hands folded carefully on her lap as John started the engine, then taxied the plane to a runway. He spoke into his radio headset, then sent the plane racing down the runway. Rachel closed her eyes as they lifted into the air.

When she opened them again, they were still climbing, and all she could see through the windshield were clouds. They leveled off, but Rachel jumped when the plane bucked once.

"Just a little turbulence," John said soothingly, his eyes focused straight ahead. "We're crossing the river now. Look at the flooding."

She dutifully looked in the direction he was pointing. At that spot the Mississippi River looked more like a spreading lake than a river. As they flew over the area, Rachel looked down and saw electric poles and rooftops poking above the waterline. It looked eerily peaceful from above, like looking down into some giant aquarium decorated with toy houses.

She didn't realize that her hands were gripping the seat belt until John glanced at her and frowned. "Are you still afraid of small places?" he asked, not unkindly.

Rachel nodded. It was a minor affliction, but one that had stayed with her since childhood. When her mother brought men home, she had told Rachel to stay in her bedroom. It was a small bedroom on the north side with one tiny window. Listening to the sounds of laughter coming from the other bedroom, Rachel had put her hands over her ears, feeling the walls closing in on her.

"Look over there," John said, pointing down at the river again.

Rachel looked and saw the lock and dam, one of several along the river. "The bald eagles hunt for fish there," he said. "Look, there goes one."

Fascinated, Rachel watched the bird soar and glide, the wind currents lifting him in circles.

John told her about the other wildlife along the river and then retold the stories from the glory days of the river when steamboats and gamblers reigned and a change of fortune was only as far away as the next ace of diamonds.

Gradually her hands released their grip and her back relaxed against the seat. She could see the people John talked about with such vivid detail. His great-grandfather had been a captain on a riverboat, and Rachel could imagine him looking much like John—big, dark, imposing, dashing. He must have cut quite a figure.

John stopped his story and began talking into his headset. Looking around curiously, Rachel saw that they were approaching a small airport straight ahead. The plane had been slowly dropping in altitude, but John's stories had kept her from noticing. She looked at her watch and realized they must be almost in St. Louis.

Knowing that he was preoccupied with landing the plane, she let herself study his profile. It amazed her that he remembered she had a fear of closed-in spaces. It was even more amazing to her that he had taken the trouble to keep her mind off her fear for the entire trip.

This little regional airport was about forty miles from Lambert Field, where David would arrive. John checked in with a friend and rented a car. When they arrived at Lambert, they still had twenty minutes before David's flight landed.

Rachel headed immediately for the gate, but John took her arm and gently steered her toward a snack stand. "You haven't eaten for hours," he said. "We'll hear the announcement when the plane lands."

John got them hot dogs and nachos, practically feeding her by hand when her gaze kept straying to the waiting area.

"Come on, Rachel," he coaxed her. "Your son will have eaten lunch on the plane. You need this."

It never ceased to amaze her how solicitous John could be where her well-being was concerned. He could snarl and snap all he wanted, but the kind things he did for her belied his gruff demeanor.

She remembered his words when they made love, *It's the memory that will stay with me the rest of my life....* So many things John wouldn't come out and say to her. The most painful for her was his silent blame for their breakup. If only he would spill his anger, she could handle it. But he let it out slowly in glances, small words and sharp tones.

Still, his gentleness with her today said that he wasn't totally unforgiving.

Rachel was out of her seat and halfway down the concourse before the announcement of the flight's arrival had ended. John threw away their trash and strode after her.

She looked so eager and so... hesitant, John thought as he stood off to her side, studying her face. It was obvious how much she loved her son. John couldn't help wondering about the boy's father. Why wasn't he involved in the child's life? Surely that hadn't been Rachel's decision alone.

For all of Rachel's lover's money, he hadn't brought her any real happiness, except for her son.

He saw Rachel's face light up and then he turned automatically toward the door. A young boy with Rachel's hair, and dark blue eyes was waving to her and grinning.

Rachel's heart skipped a beat when she saw David. How like his father he looked! The same eyes, the same smile. She wondered if John would see the resemblance but didn't dare look at him.

If only he hadn't been so angry, she would have told him before David arrived. She'd put it off for far too long now.

David reached her a minute later, standing shyly as she hugged him hard. She started to ruffle his hair, hesitated, then went ahead and did it.

David grinned and ducked his head.

"How was soccer camp?" she asked.

"Great! You should see how I play now."

"More awesome than ever, huh?" She put an arm around his shoulders and drew him toward John. "There's someone I want you to meet. David, this is John McClennon. John is an old friend of mine."

David smiled and stuck out his hand. "How do you do, sir."

John's eyebrows went up, and he looked at Rachel as he swallowed David's hand in his much larger one. "Please," he said, "call me John. It's a pleasure to meet you, David."

David looked at his mother as if for permission to use the informal name, and she nodded, smiling.

"Thank you, John," he said.

He chattered to his mother about camp all the way down the concourse to the baggage-claim area, and John hung back, marveling at the two of them. So Rachel wasn't the permissive type. He had to admit that from first impressions she'd done a great job with David. He was an engaging boy with Rachel's innocent expression and mischievous sparkle.

He was talkative, too, and Rachel indulged him on the ride to the smaller airport, her eyes alight as she turned around in the front seat to question him about camp. "You didn't eat too much junk food, did you?"

David grinned. "Gee, Mom, a guy can't keep track of every Twinkie."

"That's what mothers are for," she informed him.

The late-afternoon sun was warming the car, and Rachel slipped off her sweater. John watched her covertly. She was more relaxed than he'd seen her since they'd made love. He supposed he was mostly to blame for that. He'd done a pretty good job of jumping down her throat every chance he got.

David looked around in interest as they pulled into the small airport's parking lot. "Hey, what's this?" he asked.

"John's flying us back to Pierce," Rachel said.

"Really? You're a pilot?" David leaned forward, his eyes bright.

John smiled. "Licensed and everything. Come on in with me, and I'll show you how we file a flight plan."

"Cool! You coming, Mom?"

"No, I think I'll wait for you here." She watched the two of them head for the building, David nearly skipping to keep up with John's longer strides. He looked up at John once, and the eagerness and innocence on his face made her heart clench.

He was going to be a magnificent man—like his father. She wondered how John and David would handle the truth. She couldn't blame either of them if they were furious with her.

She got out of the car and wandered over to the glass front of the airport building, pretending to fool with the soda machine. She could see John and David inside, John talking to a man behind a desk and David listening avidly. The man smiled and waved them off, and the two headed for a back room.

She was leaning against the building when they returned. "You'll have to tell me how much the gas is and any...other expenses," she said, hurrying to keep up with them as John and David walked toward the tarmac.

"You don't owe me anything," John said over his shoulder, and she saw his spine stiffen.

"I can't let you do this for us out of your own pocket," she insisted, nearly running into his back when he stopped abruptly.

"Rachel, I'm capable of deciding how I want to spend my money," he told her in a low voice.

David was listening, but Rachel noticed that he pretended to study the ground.

"John, I don't want to be in your debt." She lowered her voice.

His jaw tightened. "I would never hold you to any debt, real or imagined," he said in an equally low voice. They both knew they were encompassing far more than a plane ride now.

She was nearly whispering when she answered. "Maybe if you did, you wouldn't be so angry."

John didn't say anything, just stared back at her, his eyes turbulent and unreadable. Finally he turned away and opened the plane door. He took Rachel's arm and helped her climb up.

"Will you be all right in the back seat?" he asked politely, but she heard the edge in his voice.

"Yes, fine."

David was momentarily silenced by the scene he had witnessed, but John took pains to put him at ease while he readied the plane for takeoff.

Once they were in the air, John explained the controls to David, and Rachel leaned forward to listen, her arm resting on the top of David's seat. John reached over, his fingers touching her in a reassuring gesture.

"Are you all right?" he asked.

"Yes," she said around the lump in her throat.

He glanced back at her, then, apparently satisfied that she was telling the truth, he began talking to David again.

Rachel sat back, the touch of John's fingers still warm and sensual on her arm. *John David McClennon,* she thought in despair, *why are you doing this to me?* She would almost rather he yell at her than show her this tenderness. Each time he was gentle with her, she almost grew weak from the need for him to hold her.

She couldn't let herself feel these things for John. She had his son, and she had to steel herself to tell him. She was already emotionally drained just from facing John again. If she let herself acknowledge how deeply she cared for him, she would never get over the inevitable heartache to come.

David had been captivated by the entire plane ride—and by John. They had flown up the river with John telling David many of the same stories he'd told Rachel on the way down. He pointed out landmarks, gave a history of the steamboats and of the Native Americans and traders who first settled on the river.

Occasionally, John would turn to Rachel to make sure she was all right. She smiled to reassure him, but she wasn't all right at all. She was feeling a claustrophobia of a different sort. It was painful to be so near John, to watch him interact with *their* son and know that she had deceived him. If not for her, there might have been other days like this, father and son enjoying time together.

But she couldn't have told him about David while he was married, she told herself. Then another person would have been hurt, as well. And Rachel would have been repeating her mother's history.

They were pulling up to the farmhouse now. David, exhausted, was sleeping between them in the truck, his head on Rachel's shoulder. After landing in Pierce, they had stopped for some ice cream and then John had given David a brief tour of the area before heading home.

It was dusk, and David had fallen asleep to the sounds of the frogs and crickets, the first time he had heard the sounds of the countryside.

John reached for David after he stopped the truck, but Rachel put a hand on his arm. "John," she whispered, "you should drop us off at the cabin."

John didn't say anything, just gave her a stony look and gathered the boy into his arms.

Rachel followed him into the house and upstairs to a spare bedroom. He laid David on the bed, covered him with a sheet, then walked past her and down the stairs without looking back.

Rachel hesitated, standing in the doorway and watching her son sleep. Then, reluctantly, she turned and followed John.

No matter how painful, it was time they talked.

Seven

Rachel stopped in the doorway and silently watched John prowl the kitchen. He grabbed a beer from the refrigerator and leaned against a counter, popping open the can. His back was to her.

"John, David and I can't stay here," she said quietly. She was tired, and her voice had grown more hoarse as the day wore on.

He turned slowly, taking a long drink from the can and regarding her with steely eyes.

"Not after what happened today...in Jake's cabin," she said when he didn't answer.

"You can't go back to your cabin until I fix the roof," he told her flatly. "I can start on it tomorrow."

"It's not the cabin roof, and we both know it." When he turned his back on her again, she grasped his arm. "John, we have to talk about what happened."

"I'm not interested in talking," he said forcefully, pulling away from her and slamming down the can so that beer sloshed onto the counter. He rounded on her, his fingers closing on her arms. "What is it you want, Rachel? Do you want me to make love to you again so you can prove just how far I'll go before you leave me? How many times do I have to play the fool?"

"It isn't that at all," she said miserably. But she shivered as she thought of the pleasure his lovemaking had brought her. He must have felt the involuntary movement, because he abruptly released her and backed up to the counter.

"The hell it isn't," he ground out. "If you came back here to prove something, I'm not going to be any part of it. Why don't you go play games with your son's father?"

Rachel nearly said the words, the pronouncement that would stop John cold. But she couldn't. Not when he was in such anguish. Not when the truth would cause him even more pain.

"I told you," she said huskily. "David's father doesn't see us anymore."

"Did you leave him, too, Rachel?"

When she didn't answer, John reached out and lifted her chin with his finger. His eyes probed hers.

"Things didn't work out, John. That's all there is to it." It was only partially a lie. Things certainly hadn't worked out between her and David's father.

He studied her face a long moment in silence before the anger began to drain from him. "What was he like, Rachel? What kind of man wouldn't fight to be with you and his son?" John's hand under her chin gentled, his thumb slowly caressing her cheek.

Rachel felt her heart contract.

"He's a very kind, very decent man," she said, trying to keep her voice even. "Don't blame him. I made the decision."

"Why?"

"Because I didn't want to hurt him."

She'd gone over her reasons so many times in her mind that she felt a vague sense of déjà vu, as if she'd had this argument with John in the past.

John shook his head. "Rachel, I don't think you have any idea how much you've probably hurt David's father with your decision."

"I *do* know, John," she whispered, her lips trembling. "I know all too well."

"Then why did you do it?"

"Because I had to," she said simply. "If I'd done what I wanted—what I needed—I would have ruined his life."

"I can't believe that," he murmured, his voice strained, but he could see from her tortured expression that she certainly believed it. He didn't want to see Rachel in such pain. He closed his eyes, his hands helplessly touching her shoulders, drawing her toward him.

I can't do this, he thought wildly. I can't let both of us go on hurting each other this way. But he couldn't stop himself. When he was near Rachel, his body ached for her so much that nothing else seemed to matter, the past—her betrayal, his anger.

It was more than a physical need, no matter how much he claimed that that was all it was. There was something deep inside him that yearned for her, some vestige of the boy who had adored her and had wanted nothing more than to protect her and make her happy.

One hand slipped into her hair as he tilted her head back and lowered his mouth. A fraction of a second before he kissed her he saw the same consuming ache in her eyes that he felt deep inside.

She whispered against his mouth, whether it was his name or a moan, he wasn't sure. It didn't matter. What they had to say to each other, what was really important, was said in this.

He thought of the man who had kissed her like this before, who had slept with her and given her a son, and he felt a sharp stab of jealousy. But, from what she said, it was over, and he couldn't dwell on it or he would go mad.

John let his mouth feed him on sweet kisses against her neck as he inhaled the woman scent of her. He silently berated himself for wanting more, but that's how it had always been with him and Rachel. He had never had enough of her. Even as a boy he couldn't wait for the next time he would see her.

Tonight, though, he reminded himself that her son was upstairs sleeping, that he was a man now and he could restrain himself. "You'd better get some rest," he told her in a hoarse voice, pulling away to look into her face.

When the kiss ended, her eyes, so beautiful to him, faded to a dull, haunted look. He pressed his hand lightly to her forehead.

"You've been coughing all day again, and you feel hot. Maybe I should call Mom and get you to a doctor."

Rachel shook her head. "I'm just a little keyed up from seeing David again. I'll be all right. Shall I sleep in . . ."

"My room," he directed smoothly. "I'll take the room near David's. He won't know where he is when he wakes up. You sleep, and I'll take care of him."

"John," she said when he was about to turn away. "Thank you for everything."

"It was nothing," he said. "Good night."

She watched him take a long sip of his beer before she turned and climbed the stairs. She felt empty inside, because what had happened between her and John was a lot more than nothing to her.

Rachel woke the next morning when the clock radio came on beside her bed in the early hours. She vaguely remembered hearing the shower earlier. She still felt bone tired, and she lay there, half dozing, listening to the news.

The rain up north had stopped, and the river was expected to crest at thirty feet in two days.

Struggling out of bed, she dressed in the clothes she'd worn the day before and checked on David from his bedroom doorway. He was still sleeping, his arm thrown over the pillow beside him, his hair tousled.

She knew how exhausted he must be. Camp had ended just the day before he'd flown here, and then there was the long trip by himself. He was quite a kid, she thought in pride. He had a maturity beyond his years.

"He woke up once last night," John said quietly behind her, and Rachel turned quickly. He was so close that she could smell the clean, soapy scent from his morning shower.

Flustered, she quickly closed David's door and moved away from John. She started coughing and miserably wished her cold would just go away.

"He got up once last night looking for the bathroom," John said. "I got him settled and explained where he was."

Rachel realized that she must have been tired not to have heard David.

"We'll go to the cabin as soon as he gets up," she said.

"You need more rest," John told her. "Go back to bed. You look exhausted, and you sound awful. Jordan came over for breakfast. He'll stay here in case David wakes up while you're sleeping."

"I don't think I can sleep anymore," she said honestly. "I'll feel better if I get moving."

"I'm going over to the cabin after I eat," he said. "You might as well go back to bed."

"I'll go with you. I need to fix up some things before David moves in."

"You're really going through with this, aren't you?" he demanded.

"If you mean moving into the cabin and living here, yes, I am."

"And what if your son's father comes looking for the two of you and wants you to come back with him?"

"That won't happen," she said, avoiding John's eyes.

"How can you guarantee that?"

"I can," she said with certainty, starting down the stairs before he could come up with more questions about David's father.

In the kitchen, she busied herself helping Jordan fix breakfast. They were talking about the predicted flood crest when John came downstairs. He grabbed his toolbox and started for the door without saying anything.

Rachel looked up from buttering some toast. "Wait, John, you haven't eaten anything."

"I'm not hungry."

Jordan was watching him with a frown. "Why am I cooking this big breakfast if you're not eating?" he demanded. "And where are you going, anyway?"

"I have to work on the roof at Rachel's cabin. I'll eat later."

"I'm going with you," Rachel said decisively, snatching up several pieces of toast and running after him as he banged out the door. "Jordan, would you let David know where we are?" she called over her shoulder.

"Yeah, sure," Jordan called back. Then he grinned to himself. "So big brother's on the run," he said with a chuckle.

Rachel practically ran to the truck, afraid John might just leave without her if she wasn't fast enough. He certainly didn't seem to want to be with her today. She didn't wait to see if he would help her into the truck but climbed up unaided. She sat and nibbled her toast, listening to him load the ladder into the back.

When he slid in beside her, she handed him a piece of toast, and John took it without comment. His fingers briefly brushed hers, and both of them jerked away as if burned.

She couldn't do this, she thought for the hundredth time. She couldn't stay here and be near him like this. She would go mad with want.

John had gone up into the crawl space above the ceiling to locate the leak, and Rachel had found herself stopping to listen to the sounds of him moving around carefully up there. She tried to work at cleaning, but she was too distracted to accomplish much.

She had made coffee when he came down, covered with dirt and cobwebs, and he quickly swallowed a cupful without comment. Then he put the ladder against the cabin and climbed up on the roof. He'd been there the last hour and a half, pulling off shingles and pitching them to the ground.

Rachel scrubbed the kitchen floor to the rhythmic thud of shingles hitting earth. As she worked, she made a mental list of the things she needed in town.

The work tired her quickly, and Rachel sat down at the kitchen table to rest. It took several minutes before her cough subsided. She was out of shape, she told herself. Her apartment hadn't required much cleaning, and she wasn't used to this much physical activity.

John glanced at her sharply when he came in, then began washing his hands and arms at the kitchen sink.

Rachel felt her mouth go dry as she stared, fascinated, at his arm muscles as he moved. She stood abruptly, needing to put some distance between them.

"I have to buy some linens," she said. "I won't be long."

"I'll go with you."

"What?" Rachel stopped in dismay. She had wanted to get away from him, not share the trip.

John's eyebrows rose when he turned to face her. "Sorry to disappoint you. But I need shingles and roofing cement."

"I'm not disappointed. I . . ." She didn't finish the sentence in the face of his skeptical look. "Maybe I shouldn't leave," she said. "I don't want David to come up when no one's here."

"Jordan won't let him if he sees that your car's gone."

"I didn't know you could see the car from your farm," she said, then stopped when she saw his expression alter.

"I can see the whole cabin from my bedroom." He clenched his jaw and turned away so she wouldn't see his face. But it was too late. She'd already read the hunger there.

He'd watched the cabin the first night she was here, she realized. It made her feel even more edgy to know that he'd been thinking about her the way she had been thinking about him.

She was so hopelessly besotted with him that she was reacting like a child, she chided herself.

Rachel snatched up her purse and car keys and fled to the car, John following her silently. Her fingers trembled as she started the car, and she looked everywhere except at John.

There had always been a hardware store on the main street of Pierce, though it had changed hands numerous times over the years. Rachel automatically headed in that direction.

She had forgotten that she had to drive past the grade school. It looked much the same except for a small new addition on the back. It was a cafeteria, she realized as she turned the corner.

The old cafeteria had been so woefully small that there were four lunch shifts to accommodate all the children. The food had been good, at least to Rachel's modest taste buds, but more often than not she had to make do with smelling it rather than eating. Her mother had a habit of borrowing back Rachel's lunch money if she was going out drinking.

If there was enough bread and peanut butter in the house, Rachel made a decent enough lunch for herself. But often the house was too food poor to come up with a meal, and Rachel went without. That was, until John David McClennon realized what was happening.

He began quizzing her each day about what she had for lunch, and if he sensed that she was lying, he would order her to show him her lunch money or her sandwich. If she couldn't produce either, he gave her half his lunch. Soon he was bringing two full lunches each day, and Rachel was expected to eat one of them.

And when John moved on to junior high school, he still found some excuse to walk past her bus stop each morning to make sure she had a lunch.

He had been her best friend, and he had cared for her so much then.

Rachel didn't realize that she was crying until the street blurred in front of her.

"What's wrong?" John asked, concern lacing his voice as she quickly swiped at her eyes. His fingers touched her arm, making her hands tremble all the more.

Afraid that she would run into something, she pulled the car to the curb and stopped. John handed her a handkerchief, and she wiped her eyes until she could control her sniffling.

"Blow your nose," he ordered her, and she complied. "Feel better?"

Rachel nodded her head. She still didn't dare look at him. "I'm sorry. I guess it's the strain of coming back here and then this cold." She shrugged her shoulders.

John's hand was gentle as his fingers touched her cheek and drew her face toward him.

"Was it the school?"

She hesitated, then nodded. "I thought I'd put all those memories behind me, but passing the school caught me unawares." She managed to meet his eyes. "Sometimes I think I wouldn't have made it without you when I was a kid."

"You forget," he said softly. "You did just as much for me."

Rachel shook her head.

John smiled, and she found she couldn't look away from him. When he treated her tenderly, she had no defenses.

"I was the boy with the hand-me-down clothes that Jake had practically worn to threads by the time I got them. I had to do chores in the morning, and I came to school with mud—or worse—on my shoes. Don't you remember how the kids used to tease me and how you stuck up for me?"

Rachel frowned. "Why did they pick on you?" she wondered aloud. "You certainly weren't the only boy who lived on a farm."

John's brows went up. "Don't you remember? The year you started first grade the new elementary school was built farther out in the county. The farm kids all went to it. But by some quirk of geography, our farm was right on the district line. I ended up here, just about the only farm kid."

No, she hadn't remembered. But now she knew why they had felt such a bond at an early age. They were both outsiders, she because of her mother's reputation and behavior, John because of his background and poverty.

"I can still recall you taking a poke at a boy twice your
size when he made fun of my shoes at recess," John said,
grinning. "I thought you were about the bravest and pret-
tiest thing I'd ever seen."

That made Rachel smile, that John had thought her
brave. She figured he'd thrown in the pretty to be kind. She
had been more than a little ragged in those days, with no
mother around to wash and brush her hair or to iron her
clothes. Rachel had done it herself after a fashion, but it was
a long while before she got very good at it.

"You were the best friend a kid could want," she told him
honestly.

"It was always more than just friendship with us, wasn't
it?" he said quietly.

She couldn't meet his eyes anymore and dropped hers.
"Yes."

"From the day I met you I felt incomplete when you
weren't with me," he said. "I couldn't put it into words
then, but I felt it."

Rachel nodded. It had been the same for her.

Slowly John withdrew his hand. "Time changes things,
doesn't it?"

"I suppose it does." She had to work to keep the tears
from her voice. Time had changed a lot of things, but not
how she felt about John. No matter how angry he was with
her, she still felt such need for him that it threatened to
overwhelm her.

She wanted to tell him about his son, but when she
glanced at his face and saw the implacable set of his jaw she
knew she couldn't do it then. But soon. She had to tell him
soon. No matter the cost.

"Turn here," John said gently when they reached the
main street in town. "There's a new mall a mile on the right.
It's practically driven all the older, smaller stores out of
business."

"I guess everyone has to change with the times," she said
quietly, thinking that she was a fool for not changing with
them herself. She still loved John, as useless as that senti-

ment was now. She was hanging on to a past that had vanished in the face of her lie.

"You can't stop change," John said ruefully, and when she glanced at him, she saw the sadness back in his eyes.

Rachel realized when she saw the mall that she must have passed it on her way into town, but then she hadn't been paying that much attention to her surroundings. John David McClennon had been on her mind as always.

She and John headed in opposite directions in the discount department store, Rachel for linens and John for hardware.

Half an hour later she was finished and looking for John when she saw him in a checkout lane, talking rapidly with Jake. There was such a sense of urgency about the conversation that she began walking toward them. John saw her and gave Jake a warning look.

"What's wrong?" Rachel asked.

Jake exchanged glances with John. "I need to borrow John for a little bit, Rachel. Could you drive on home alone?"

Rachel looked from one man to the other anxiously. "Is David all right?" she demanded on a rising note of worry.

"Yes, David's fine," John assured her. "This has nothing to do with him."

Rachel quickly put two and two together. "Then it has to be Mason, right? What's happened? Is he okay?"

John looked at Jake in wry defeat. "I told you you can't get anything past Rachel. We might as well bring her along."

Jake shrugged, but he was watching Rachel worriedly. "Rachel, promise me you'll stay in the truck."

"No," Rachel said, heading for the door.

It was strange how swiftly childhood emotions could swirl to the surface, given the right circumstances. And these had sure been the right circumstances, Rachel thought wryly as she glanced in the rearview mirror of the truck.

Mason had gone off the wagon big-time, and after a prolonged bout of drinking he had become belligerent in the bar. The owner, knowing the family, had called Jake instead of the police. The bar wasn't far from the mall, so when Jake found out where John was, he had come looking for him to help corral Mason.

Rachel had stood in the doorway and been treated to the sight of her aggressive, falling-down-drunk brother being forcibly hauled away by Jake and John.

Now she drove the truck while the two brothers held Mason down in the truck bed. *The acorn doesn't fall far from the tree,* she thought bitterly. How many times had she stood at the kitchen window and watched some strange man bring home her inebriated mother?

But this was her brother, and the men bringing him home were dear friends of hers. Tears came to her eyes, but she forced them back. She wouldn't let Mason see what this was doing to her.

John had insisted that she drive to the farm instead of Mason's apartment, and Rachel stopped the truck in the drive, wondering how she was going to explain this to David. "Your uncle's drunk on his butt—just like your grandmother used to be." Shuddering, she stepped down and slammed the door.

"I am not through partying, man," Mason announced loudly as John and Jake hauled him to his feet and maneuvered him out of the back of the truck.

"Wrong, man, you're definitely through," Jake said through gritted teeth. "Now get in the damn house."

Mason put up token resistance, then started laughing as he let Jake lead him up the steps and through the door where Jordan was waiting.

Rachel followed them and stood in the hallway as Jordan took over for John and helped Jake guide Mason to a back bedroom. When she turned around, she saw David watching from the kitchen doorway, his mouth trembling. But before she could move, John went to him.

"I'm sorry about the noise, son," John said, his hand lightly coming to rest on David's shoulder. "Your uncle Mason's had a little too much to drink."

"Will he be all right?" David asked, staring up at John.

"He'll feel like hell when the alcohol wears off," John told him. "And it's going to be rough for him not to take another drink, but I think he'll be all right. If I know my brother, Jake's liable to choke him if he even thinks about a drink."

"Why's he want another drink if it makes him feel so lousy?" David asked.

John glanced at Rachel, who was hugging her arms to herself, then led David into the kitchen. "You, too," he said to Rachel over his shoulder. She followed reluctantly, still feeling raw and embarrassed by the scene she'd witnessed.

John pulled out a chair for her, his hand brushing her shoulder, deliberately she suspected, as she sat. He got a can of soda for each of them and sat down between her and David.

"Mason has a problem," John told David. "He can't help wanting to drink, and when he starts, he can't stop. It's an illness. It's very hard for him not to drink. He fights it all the time, and today he lost one of the battles."

"Why'd he lose it today?" David asked matter-of-factly.

"He has a friend who talked him into going into the tavern," John told him, his eyes sliding to Rachel's. "She has a problem with alcohol, too, but she's not fighting it as hard as Mason is."

"Oh," David said, as if understanding had just dawned. "Like peer pressure."

John smiled. "That's right. Mason gave in to peer pressure today."

"Yeah." David took a drink of his soda and shrugged. "That happens sometimes."

"What's Mason's friend's name?" Rachel asked John quietly.

He studied her a moment before answering. "Lisa Harmon. She's Tiny's daughter. He's fit to be tied."

Rachel could imagine. The girl had to be a teenager. And Tiny, a kind, generous man, would be horribly embarrassed by her behavior. Just as Rachel had been by her mother's behavior and now by Mason's.

"I need to talk to Mason," she said suddenly, standing and giving David a hug because she felt as if she needed one herself, desperately.

"Rachel . . ." John began.

"Just for a minute," she said. "To see if he's all right."

Jake and Jordan were just leaving the bedroom as Rachel arrived. Mason was lying on top of the bedspread, moaning. "God, I don't know how this happened," he groaned.

"We'll talk about it later," Jake said, eyeing Rachel with a frown. "Are you sure you want to see him now?" he asked softly.

Rachel nodded, and the two brothers hesitated a moment before going on down the hall toward the kitchen.

"Hey, how're you feeling?" Rachel asked, sitting on the edge of the bed.

Mason pulled his arm from over his eyes, then dropped it back in place. "Like a cat in a washing machine," he said hoarsely, his speech slurred. "Hell, Rachel, I drank almost a quart of whiskey on a dare. How do you think I feel?"

"I'm surprised you can feel anything," she said honestly.

"Which is the main reason I drink," he said, flinging his arm out for emphasis and nearly hitting her in the process. "So I won't feel."

Sadly, Rachel could understand that reason quite well.

When she didn't say anything, Mason opened his eyes and fixed her with a bleary gaze. "Don't mess up your life like I did, Rachel."

"You're young, and your life isn't ruined by any means," Rachel reassured him, but he grabbed her hand and held on tight.

"You have a good job, a good life. You've got a kid, Rachel. Hell, you've got John McClennon's kid, and if that isn't a reason to be happy, then—"

"Mason, shh!" Rachel shushed him, anxiously looking at the doorway. "Please! John doesn't know and neither does David."

"Why not?" Mason asked, then shrugged and dropped her hand as if the question had quickly lost all importance. "Lisa wants a baby," he said wearily, his eyes closing again.

Rachel chewed her lip. "Mason, you didn't say anything about David to Lisa, did you?"

But Mason was moaning again and lost in his misery.

Rachel watched him a moment with a worried frown, then sighed and stood. She wouldn't get any more conversation from him tonight.

She prayed that if Lisa Harmon knew about David, she would forget when she came out of her alcoholic haze.

When Rachel got back to the kitchen, the brothers were pulling on windbreakers and boots. She glanced outside and saw the rain hitting the window. It was a hard rain, not a gentle misting but a gully washer that would cause problems.

David was sitting quietly at the table, watching the men's preparations.

"I'll bring you some coffee," she offered worriedly.

John shook his head. "Stay here with Mason and David. See if you can get Mason to sleep. Jake and Jordan are going to pick up your car, then come back here to work on the levee." He studied her face, then abruptly rummaged in the cabinet and brought out a bottle of cough syrup. "Take some of this and rest yourself. You need it."

But Rachel, exhausted as she was, knew that she would not be able to sleep. Not when the levee hung in the balance again.

Jake and Jordan were already out the door when John came back and stood in front of her. He looked her in the eyes for a long moment, and then his big hand cupped the back of her head and his mouth came down on hers. It was a swift, gentle kiss, but it left her shaken as he turned and hurried out the door before she had time to draw another breath.

She flushed and glanced over at David to find him smiling shyly.

She tried to think of something to tell David, but nothing came to mind but the truth. *John's your father, and I think I still love him.*

No, she couldn't tell him that.

Eight

Rachel checked on Mason and, satisfied that he was sound asleep, returned to the kitchen. Needing to keep busy, she got a couple of mugs from the cupboard and set about making hot chocolate for David and herself.

"Is Mr. McClennon—John—the friend you've always talked about?" David asked.

Rachel's fingers slipped on the milk she was pulling from the refrigerator, but she recovered and set it on the counter, her heart beating madly.

"Yes," she said, turning to face David. "I didn't think you'd remember."

David grinned. "Come on, Mom. You always said he was your best friend. And just now he kissed you like—" David stopped in embarrassment, then shrugged. "I mean, it's not hard to see you guys got a thing for each other."

"David, John and I don't have a *thing*." She flushed. At least John didn't, she amended to herself. "We're good friends."

"Right," David said, but he was grinning, and it was clear that he enjoyed seeing his mother in this new light, a woman with a *thing*.

The hot chocolate had been drunk, lunch had been eaten and Rachel and David were cleaning up the dishes when Elizabeth arrived, breathless and tired.

She hugged David when he was introduced, then nodded her head toward the back room in a silent question.

"Mason's asleep," Rachel said. "My guess is he will be for quite a while."

Elizabeth shook her head and sank down on a kitchen chair. "Jake told me. And he was doing so well."

"Getting this far, admitting that he has a problem, is a big step for him," Rachel said, realizing that it was the truth, a truth she hadn't realized before now. Mason was waging his own personal battle, and her embarrassment for him was unwarranted because, unlike their mother, he was trying.

"Yes, it is," Elizabeth said absently, frowning as she studied Rachel's face. "Rachel, you don't look well. Are you sure you're all right?"

Rachel smiled and nodded. "Just tired. And a lingering cold."

"My son isn't giving you trouble?"

"Your son always gives me trouble," Rachel returned, making Elizabeth smile.

"He kissed Mom," David offered, shrugging as Rachel gave him a dark look.

"Did he, now?" Elizabeth said with interest. "And what do you make of that, David?"

"I figure they've got a thing for each other. But Mom says they're just friends."

"Hmm," Elizabeth acknowledged knowingly, grinning at Rachel.

"It's not what you think," Rachel said, though she knew her protest was in vain. Elizabeth was clearly happy that her son had kissed Rachel. Rachel only wished that the kiss had meant what Elizabeth and David assumed it meant.

But she knew what John's intent had been. He was sorry that he'd been so abrupt with her, and he was sorry that Mason had fallen off the wagon and Rachel had witnessed it. In short, he felt sorry for her.

And pity was never what she'd wanted from John Mc-Clennon.

"Have you had lunch?" Rachel asked.

Elizabeth shook her head. "No, but I have to leave. I just came by to give you the news. A section of the levee just south of the Cedarwood break is soft, and the National Guard is evacuating this whole area. I'm on my way to tell the boys."

Rachel knew that the boys were her sons, and the news was bad. The National Guard had been working on the north levees for several days now. The sound of helicopters flying overhead was an hourly occurrence. If they were evacuating the farms, that meant that they couldn't make the levee strong enough for the rising water. She glanced around the kitchen worriedly, thinking about all the memories here that could fall prey to the water if the levee broke.

"You stay here and eat something," Rachel told Elizabeth. "I'll go to the levee and give them the news. Can you stay with David?"

"Sure, honey, but your voice sounds awful," Elizabeth protested.

Rachel shook her head. "I'll be all right. Just let me grab some sandwiches to take."

Over Elizabeth's protests, Rachel quickly made up some bologna sandwiches and stuffed them into a picnic cooler that the men had left by the door. She added three six-packs of soda and took off. David had wanted to come along, but Rachel worried about taking him to the levee when things sounded so perilous.

She was right to worry, she thought, when she drew within sight of the workers' faces. They were grim and tired, and there was little talking.

Rachel was out of breath from coughing and from walking so far with her load. She'd parked her car well away from the levee. She set down the cooler to take a deep breath, and another coughing spell racked her, leaving her bent over with her hands on her knees.

"What are you doing out here?" an angry voice demanded, and she looked up into John's scowling face.

"I brought you some food and soda," she said, but before she could go on with the evacuation news, she was coughing again.

John knelt beside her and pressed the back of his hand to her forehead. "You're hot."

"Of course I'm hot," she said. "It's eighty degrees and muggy as hell. And I walked half a mile from my car lugging this stuff. So you'd better eat a sandwich, John McClennon, or I'm liable to—" She didn't finish as she started coughing again.

"You're not liable to do anything but collapse," John ground out. "If I didn't have this levee to worry about, I'd take you and—" He abruptly stopped speaking, his face flushed as if the thought of what he wanted to do to her was more than he could handle at the moment. "Get in my truck and lie down," he muttered gruffly.

"Wait, John," she said, putting her hand on his arm when he started to walk away. She felt his muscle jump beneath her touch. "Your mother came by. There's a problem with the levee north of here. The National Guard is evacuating this area."

John glanced over his shoulder as if he would see the floodwaters racing toward him that moment. "Just what we need," he said wearily. "Another levee break."

Jake, Jordan, Tiny and the five other workers were dropping their sandbags and walking slowly toward Jake and Rachel. It was painfully obvious that everyone was bone tired.

"Sandwiches!" Tiny said with satisfaction as he opened the cooler. He pulled out two and popped open a soda, lowering himself to the wet ground with a tired grunt.

"Don't get too comfortable," John warned him. "Rachel says the National Guard is evacuating this area."

Jake swore. "We've got to finish this section before we leave."

John nodded. "I know. It won't hold if we don't. Let's go." He signaled to the men and raised his voice. "Grab a sandwich and let's get back to work. We don't have much time."

Rachel started to follow him, but John turned to face her, his hands on his hips. "Wait in the truck," he ordered her in a quiet voice. She was tempted to follow him anyway, but when she met his eyes, she saw the gravity of the situation mirrored there. "If I need you, I'll come get you," he promised, his voice still gruff.

Rachel acquiesced, going to the truck and curling up on the front seat. The windows were open, and the hot air settled over her like a blanket. She would rest a while, she told herself, then she would go back to the cabin so Elizabeth could be on her way.

When Rachel woke up, the sun was setting like a ripe peach sinking into the water. She could hear voices, and she sat up, dazed and worried. Through the windshield she could see a Jeep parked near the levee. Two National Guardsmen sat in it, and a man who wore what looked like a sheriff's uniform was talking to John and his workers.

She couldn't make out what was being said, until the sheriff turned to get back in the Jeep. Facing her now, his words carried. "Twenty-four hours. That's all we can give you. Then we have to make you go." The Jeep started to pull away, but Rachel caught his last words. "Good luck."

She felt as though she'd awakened to a nightmare. John had to leave the farmhouse within twenty-four hours. And if the levee didn't hold... She didn't even want to think about that.

Rachel composed her face as John came striding to the pickup truck. "You heard?" he asked softly, leaning his forearms on the open window.

Rachel nodded. He looked so tired. And so worried about her. His eyes were checking her restlessly, as if to assure himself that she was all right.

"What are you going to do?" she asked.

John glanced back at the levee. "We'll finish up what we can here, then start moving things out of our houses." He reached a hand inside and touched her shoulder, his thumb making slow circles on her neck. He cleared his throat. "How do you feel?"

"Much better. I'll go back to your house, and David and I can help your mother start packing things."

His voice still sounded angry, though his fingers continued to stroke her. "I don't want you working. You're too sick."

"You may be right," she admitted. "But I have to help, John. I owe it to your mother for all the times I came to your house and she took me in like one of her own children. And for the lunches you gave me in school." She tried to smile but didn't quite make it. "I might have starved to death without you and your mother," she said lightly.

"Now that would have been a shame," he said, his smile not quite reaching his eyes. "All right. Let me give you a lift to your car, then."

She slid over so John could get in behind the wheel. He drove her to her car, his eyes straight ahead, his hands steady on the wheel. Rachel glanced back once and saw the workers framed against the last of the sun. They still worked feverishly, laying down plastic and straw and anchoring it with sandbags.

When they reached her car, John put one hand over hers on the seat before she could get out. "Thank you," he said softly.

"For what?" she murmured, her breathing tremulous at his touch.

But apparently he wasn't going to expand on his gratitude. "Go on," he said. "And if you overwork yourself into a sick bed, you'll have me to deal with."

He made a mock fist at her, and Rachel leaned over quickly to brush her lips across the fist. She got out of the truck. She wasn't sure, but she thought she heard him groan softly just before she shut the door.

* * *

Rachel, David and Elizabeth had been packing dishes and clothes for two hours when John arrived at the house with Jake and Jordan in tow.

"I sent everyone else to help Tiny move his stuff," John said. "How's Mason?"

"Still sleeping it off," Elizabeth said. She nodded toward the hall, and in the ensuing silence they could hear soft snoring.

"I bet he'll wish he could remove his head when he wakes up," John said dryly.

"I'll make sure he does," Jake said with certainty.

John and his brothers began moving the appliances from the house and into the pickup truck. "Do you have enough room in your apartment for these?" Jake asked when the truck was full.

Before Elizabeth could answer, Rachel said, "Take them to the cabin. There's hardly any furniture there. You can use it for storage."

Jake looked back at John, who had just walked in and was slowly dusting off his hands. John nodded, looking more tired than Rachel could remember. It was all she could do not to run to him and put her arms around him.

"Thank you, Rachel," he said quietly.

"Yes, dear," Elizabeth said, putting an arm around Rachel's shoulders. "Thank you."

Rachel went back to packing, knowing that she could never repay the love and kindness John and his family had shown her in the past. And she could never make it up to John for what she had done to him.

She glanced over at David, feeling a sudden ache in her heart. He was carrying a box of photographs, trailing after John importantly. She wandered to the window, watching as John took the box at the truck and gave David a smile and a few words. Grinning, David hurried back to the house for another box.

He and David would have been so good together, she thought. Why haven't I told John?

Because she was terrified of what his reaction might be. She was afraid he would never want to see her or David again. She blamed herself. John would be more than justified to reject them. But she was the only one who deserved the blame. She didn't want her son hurt.

"Are you okay?" Elizabeth asked from behind her, and Rachel turned quickly, trying to smile.

"Just worried about... the levee," she said.

Elizabeth nodded, but Rachel could feel the older woman's eyes on her as she went back to work. And when David headed out the door again, Elizabeth watched him, then studied Rachel thoughtfully. Studiously, Rachel avoided meeting her eyes.

"Rachel—" Elizabeth began, but Rachel stood and headed for the back bedroom.

"I need to get some things," she said vaguely, giving Elizabeth no chance to ask what was on her mind. Whatever it was, Rachel was sure she had no ready answer for Elizabeth.

When she got to the room where Mason was sleeping, she leaned against the doorframe and caught her breath. Mason gave a loud snore and changed position, groaning in his sleep.

Rachel's stomach twisted as she remembered the many times her mother had slept for more than a day after drinking too much. When she was old enough that her mother couldn't keep her confined in her bedroom any longer, Rachel had taken on the role of caretaker during her mother's drinking bouts. At the age of nine, she was perpetually solemn, thinking about problems she had no capacity to solve.

One time Rachel had gone to check on her after she'd been asleep for what seemed far too long.

She'd hesitantly pushed open the door, whispering, "Mama?" A man had come toward her out of the shadows cast by the closed curtains, making her stumble backward and nearly cry out.

"Your mama's sleeping," he'd said groggily, closing the door again. The odor of liquor had been strong on his breath.

Rachel had retreated to the kitchen to fix her own dinner, her hands still shaking. From then on, she'd never gone near her mother's bedroom.

Now she watched Mason and realized how hard it had been on him, too. Their mother had not wanted a young boy, nearly a man, around when she was bringing men home, even sporadically.

While Rachel had been assigned to her bedroom, Mason had been sent out to the streets. He'd hung out wherever anyone would let him, and often those were not the most pleasant places for a boy. John's parents had taken him in as often as they could, but sometimes Rachel sensed that Mason was too proud to ask for their help.

After their mother was asleep Mason would sneak back home, and Rachel would fix him a meal. She tried to talk to him, to make some sense of what they were both going through, but Mason couldn't talk about it. They grew farther apart, until it seemed it was too painful for either of them to speak.

Rachel hadn't realized that she was crying until she felt the wetness on her cheeks. Brushing at her eyes, she crept into the bedroom and straightened the sheet covering Mason, then smoothed his hair.

When she turned, John was standing in the doorway. Carefully, she composed her face before she reached him. She didn't want John feeling sorry for her.

"What's done is done," he murmured softly. "The past can't hurt you anymore." Gently he drew her into his arms and held her.

Rachel released a long, pent-up sigh, clinging to his shirt and soaking up as much of his comfort as she could. "I never could fool you, could I?" she whispered ruefully.

"Yes, you could," he said, no anger in his voice. "Sometimes I didn't know who you were. You were a stranger to me."

She knew he meant the time she had left him.

"I think you're wrong," she said, drawing a deep breath and looking up at him. "I think the past can hurt both of us—very badly."

Slowly John let his eyes move over her. So slender and still so beautiful. Resilient and strong. But she was right. He still harbored anger toward her for leaving him the way she did, for taking up with another man who gave her a child. It wasn't the white-hot anger of old, but it was still there inside him, like a persistent ache.

He didn't want to care what happened to Rachel, but he did. He didn't want to see her hurt any more, even though he was the one hurting her despite himself.

Hell, he was so tired he wasn't thinking rationally at all. Firmly he held her away from him.

"It's time to go. We have to wake Mason and get out of here."

Rachel nodded and walked back to sit on the edge of the bed. "Come on, Mason," she said, gently shaking his shoulder. "It's time to go."

Mason groaned and rolled to his side. "Don't want to go," he moaned, slurring his words. "I want to stay home."

Rachel bit her lip, thinking of the times he'd had to leave the house because of their mother and seeing how the memories haunted him yet.

John was beside her the next moment. "Go wait in your car," he told her. "Jake and I'll get Mason."

Rachel got David and went to sit in her car, trying not to look a few minutes later when John and Jake came out of the house with Mason between them.

Her wayward brother. Knowing what it felt like to be abandoned, she could never do that to a child of hers.

But she'd done it to John. She'd abandoned him, and she'd done it deliberately.

He was an adult, and it had been to save him from more misery, she told herself. But seeing the look in his eyes, she knew she'd saved him no misery at all.

* * *

By the time they had finished unloading the farmhouse things at the cabin on the bluff it was almost daylight. There was precious little room to walk inside the cabin, but most of John's valuables were safe now.

David had long ago fallen into a weary sleep, and John had carried him to the bedroom, standing aside as Rachel tucked him in.

John had glanced up once at the stained ceiling, then apparently deciding that his tarp on the roof would hold for the night, he'd walked out of the room.

Now the work was done, and all that was left was to wait and see if the levee would hold. Rachel felt a sense of loss in the pit of her stomach, knowing that she and David would wait alone.

"You're exhausted," Elizabeth said to Rachel, hugging her briefly as they surveyed the room. "I can't thank you enough for what you did, Rachel."

Rachel shook her head. "I didn't do anything you wouldn't have done for me. Go on home and get some sleep yourself."

Jake and Jordan squeezed her shoulder affectionately as they passed by her on their way to the door. "You coming, John?" Elizabeth called as she moved to follow them. "I don't have any extra bedrooms, but the couch folds out into a bed."

"The couch is *mine,* " Jake said without hesitation. "I'm not sleeping in the same bed with Jordan. A guy could get hurt the way he flings his arms and legs around."

"Well, then where—" Elizabeth began.

"I'll stay here," John said. "I'm taking Rachel to the doctor as soon as the clinic opens."

Elizabeth nodded. "That's a good idea. We'll see you later, then."

"You're welcome to stay," Rachel said to John as soon as Elizabeth had gone. "But you don't have to take me to the clinic. I'm sure you're needed somewhere else." She knew she sounded formally polite, but she couldn't deal with John without some distance between them.

"No arguments," John said in a voice that meant business. "You've done this all your life, and I'm putting a stop to it."

"Done what?" she demanded.

"Put everyone else before yourself," he said. "You gave away your gloves every winter, because some other kid didn't have a pair. You gave me clothes and shoes, and I know for a fact that once you spent the grocery money your mother gave you on a sweater for me. Then you told me it was Mason's and he'd outgrown it." At her look of shock, he said, "Mason told me."

"Well, he shouldn't have," she protested, angry with both of them at the moment. "And I owed you. You gave me lunches."

John shook his head. "Don't you see, Rachel?" He stepped to her and brought her head up to meet his penetrating blue eyes. "You didn't even *have* grocery money most of the time, and when you did, you spent it on me. You took care of me the same way you took care of Mason whenever he was around. You and I didn't have any money when we were kids, and maybe that makes us different now. I don't know. But I do know that you can't make everything right with your mother by taking care of the whole world."

"I'm not—" she began sharply, but he cut her off.

"Not when you need someone to take care of you, for a change. Especially since that rich boy you fancied doesn't seem to be around to do it."

She tried to ignore the edge of sarcasm in his voice, because she felt too weary to fight with him. "Are you suggesting you're the one to do it?" she demanded with more courage than she thought she possessed.

"For tonight, honey," he told her gently. "For tonight, anyway."

Her heart fell. She should have known that he wouldn't want anything to do with her on more than a temporary basis. And once he found out about David, she might never have even that much from him.

She felt so tired suddenly, so tired and so drained that it took a supreme effort simply to put one foot in front of the other. She pulled away from John and started for the bathroom, but she didn't seem to have the energy to cross the room. Slowly she sank down on the arm of the couch.

John was by her side the next instant. "Don't fight me tonight, Rachel. Don't lead with your pride, for once in your life."

He helped her up by cupping her elbows, then threaded a path for them among the pieces of furniture. Once in the bathroom he put down the toilet seat and lowered her to sit there.

Rachel felt so dizzy that she couldn't even move as John gently washed her face.

She realized what he planned next when she saw him take her nightgown from the peg on the back of the door.

"No," she protested weakly. "I can do that myself."

John's eyes filled with amusement despite his weariness. "You're awfully cocky for someone who can barely stand up," he commented, holding the nightgown across his arm.

"I don't have to stand to undress myself," she retorted, but at the moment she seriously doubted her ability. Determined to prove otherwise to John, she leaned over to take off her shoes. She almost found herself with a close-up view of the floor tile before John caught her shoulders.

"Easy, sweetheart," he murmured, pushing her upright and quickly squatting to remove the shoes himself. She was hoping he would stop with the shoes and socks, but given John McClennon's bullheaded nature, she figured he wouldn't.

And he didn't.

He unbuttoned her blouse next, his eyes never leaving her face. By the time he slid it off her shoulders they were both breathing a little harder.

He cleared his throat before tackling her bra, and she noticed through her sleepy daze that his fingers were shaking.

"Hold still!" he ordered her in aggravation.

"I'm not the one moving," she informed him, and he cursed beneath his breath.

The bra ended up on the floor, and John's jaw clenched. For a moment he stared into her face, but then he looked away in agitation.

As quickly as he could, he unfastened her slacks and tugged them down past her hips, ignoring her protests when she couldn't lift her bottom off the seat fast enough for him. He had to reposition her to keep her from toppling off the toilet seat, and as he bent over her, their eyes met again.

She saw a sad light come into his eyes just before he drew the nightgown over her head with unnecessary force.

"You aren't very nice to me," she complained as he pushed her arms under the straps.

He gave a rueful grunt. "Do you know how hard it is *not* to be nice to you?"

"You make it look pretty darn easy from where I sit," she retorted. She was so woozy she wasn't even sure she was saying this to him, but she must be because he was studying her with a wary frown.

Rachel felt her eyes close heavily, but still she fought sleep.

He lifted her to her feet, and she could feel his hands trembling on her shoulders.

John swore softly as he saw that she was shivering. He pulled her to him, wrapping his arms around her for warmth. At least he told himself it was for warmth. The problem was, it felt too damn good to let her go. He put one arm under her knees and lifted her to his chest, his heart accelerating when she murmured his name.

He carried her to the couch in the packed living room, setting her down gently and drawing a sheet over her.

John meant to get up and go to the kitchen for some coffee, but he couldn't seem to make himself leave her when it was obvious that something was still on her mind.

She looked so fragile and pale. He stroked her blond hair from her face, longing to tangle his fingers in it while he kissed her.

He couldn't think about that now. They were both exhausted, and she was ill.

But still he couldn't stop focusing on those soft lips.

Unable to help himself, he brushed his mouth across hers, doing it again when she smiled and murmured, half-asleep. He felt his groin tighten at this simple gesture, and he made himself stop.

"Go to sleep now," he said quietly. "I'll wake you when it's time to go to the clinic."

"I can't sleep," she whispered.

John smiled despite his weariness. "I think you can if you try."

"I need to talk to you."

"What is it?"

Rachel wasn't sure if she was dreaming or if she was awake. John had kissed her. And now she had to tell him something, but she couldn't remember what it was. She fought off sleep, trying to make her mind work, but it wasn't any use. *David*. That was it. She had to make John forgive her for not telling him about his son.

Her eyes fluttered open briefly, then closed heavily again, and she groaned.

"John?" she murmured.

"What?"

"I'm sorry." It was all she could manage before she was forced to surrender to exhaustion.

She was sound asleep now, John realized. Her dark lashes were a stark contrast to her pale cheeks. He watched her a moment longer, then brushed his lips over hers again.

"I'm sorry, too, honey," he whispered.

Rachel barely woke when John took her to the clinic, David in the truck with them, and she remembered dozing on and off with her head on John's shoulder as they waited their turn. The doctor had looked down her throat, listened to her lungs and announced that she had bronchitis. She was asleep again when John drove her home in the truck.

Now she slowly surfaced from sleep, feeling groggy but much better than she had in days. When she focused her eyes, she saw John standing at the window.

"What time is it?" she asked, her voice hoarse.

John turned and picked his way around the furniture to reach the couch. "About five, I guess. How are you feeling?"

"Better. Five in the afternoon? It's so dark."

He nodded. "It's raining again. I went down once to look at the levee. I think I stopped a boil, but . . ."

He didn't say anything else and didn't meet her eyes. Rachel sighed heavily and touched his arm.

"You worked so hard," she said.

"It's not over yet." He straightened. "Come on. Time for you to take some more medicine."

Rachel swallowed the two prescription pills he held out and then the spoonful of syrup. She vaguely remembered him waking her when they'd returned to make her take medicine.

"Where's David?" she asked.

"Jordan came by and took him for a ride on his motorcycle. Is that all right?" he asked suddenly. "I didn't think you'd mind. Jordan's careful."

"It's fine. I'm grateful. I hate being useless like this." Another thought occurred to her. "Did you get any sleep?" she asked worriedly.

He nodded. "Right over there in the corner on my own couch." He gave her a rueful smile. "I've spent a lot of nights on that couch. Meredith used to give me the devil for one thing or another."

"I'm sorry."

"It's not your fault."

"I guess I gave you your share of the devil, too."

John shrugged. "It's over."

No, it isn't. He still didn't know the one thing that might hurt him more than all the rest.

Rachel squeezed his hand, wishing she could comfort him the way he had comforted her.

"Want some coffee?" John asked.

She nodded, and he stood. He was in the kitchen when someone knocked on the door. "Come in," he called.

It was Tiny, cap in hand, looking tired and agitated as he walked in. "Rachel," he said, nodding toward her. "Hope you're feeling better."

"Much better, thanks."

"John, I hate to ask," Tiny said, "but I need your help. If you ain't too busy."

"Sure, Tiny. What is it?" John set down the coffeepot and came around the counter.

"We couldn't get everything out of my house. I got a refrigerator and table left, and I can't afford to lose them. But my truck just blew a head gasket, and the rest of the boys had already left. Just got Lisa to help, and she ain't doing so hot. Hate to say it about my own daughter, but that's the way it is."

"Let's go," John said, reaching for his keys. "We can pick up Jake to help."

"We ain't got time," Tiny said in a worried voice. "John, the levee looks bad. Too soft."

John nodded grimly. "We'd better hurry then."

"Wait!" Rachel said, sitting up. "I'll go with you."

John pointed his finger at her. "You stay here. I won't have you out in the rain as sick as you are. We'll be fine," he added on a softer note.

She watched them go, twisting her hands in worry. She knew what could happen if the levee broke and trapped them. A truck was no protection. And if they couldn't get to higher ground in time...

Rachel got up and dressed in jeans and a pink pullover, then paced the room. She walked to the window and cupped her hands around her face, peering through the sheets of rain at John's farm below, trying to make out the levee from here.

Something else nagged at her as well. Lisa Harmon was with them. And Mason had told her about David. If she said something to John...

Rachel refused to even think about that.

She stared out the window for two hours, afraid to move and afraid to keep looking.

The rain was beginning to slacken when she saw it.

It was a trickle at first, almost innocent looking. Then more of the levee collapsed, and the trickle became a gushing current. Floodwater poured through the break in the levee.

Quickly she calculated in her head the distance to Tiny's farm. He was about a mile to the south of here. That meant that, unless there was another break farther south, the water wouldn't reach Tiny's place for a while, yet.

The familiar drone of a helicopter passed over the house. At least they would report the break.

Rachel's heart was pounding in her chest, but she couldn't look away. John and Tiny were out there somewhere, and the water was heading for them. She had no way to warn them, and she'd never felt so helpless in her life.

Please be safe, John, she pleaded silently. Don't leave me now. Not with things the way they are between us.

The floodwater had spread out into a solid wall. It looked so small and powerless from her vantage point. That was deceptive, because it easily toppled one tree after another, leaving only the top half of electric poles visible after it passed. It would reach John's house in a few moments.

She ran to open the door when she heard the truck. One look at John's face when he got out, and she saw that he knew. Tiny was crestfallen as both men turned to watch the water below.

Rachel went to stand beside John, and he silently put his arm around her, drawing her close. She hid her face against John's chest as the water touched his porch, unable to make herself watch the destruction of his home.

The only outward sign John gave of his emotions was a tightening of his arm on her.

She could hear the helicopter coming back upriver. Slowly she turned to face the encroaching flood. It was almost dark, but she could still see the house standing defiantly white against the gathering darkness. The first-floor windows gave under the water's pressure, the sound swallowed in the water's rush. Now the flood claimed its prize, and the house seemed to slowly descend into the murky beast.

Rachel leaned against John and began to silently cry.

Nine

Elizabeth had arrived as soon as she heard about the levee break on the radio, bringing Jake and Mason with her. Jordan showed up with David, who, despite his excitement at the motorcycle ride, grew solemn when he heard the adults discussing the levee break.

Even George and Rowena dropped by for a few minutes, offering to help any way they could.

To Rachel's relief, nightfall had obscured the farmhouse from view. After a morose few minutes spent staring out into the darkness, everyone had congregated inside wordlessly. Rachel and John had fixed sandwiches and soup.

Tiny was the most inconsolable of the group.

"That house was all I had for my daughter," he said, breaking the silence at one point. "I can't give her nothing."

"You'll rebuild," John assured him. "We'll all be back."

"I'm getting too old," Tiny said wearily. "Maybe I should just retire from farming. Lisa was such a wild girl since her mother died, and I always thought it was because she hated the farm." He glanced at Mason and then down at his plate, obviously uncomfortable.

"She has to decide what she wants on her own," Mason said, surprising everyone. He looked much the worse for wear after his drinking bout, Rachel noted. He had been silent and withdrawn since he'd arrived.

"A person can mess up their life good before they learn what it is they don't want," Mason said. His cheeks were flushed, and the speech was obviously far more than his usual conversation. "I think I'll get some air," he mumbled, rising from the table and wending his way past furniture to the door.

Jake excused himself a moment later and went to join him.

As the gathering broke up, Elizabeth offered to do the dishes so that Rachel could rest.

"You go on," John said. "I'm going to stay here with Rachel again. I don't like having her and David here with no telephone."

"All right," Elizabeth said. "But what if Jordan and I take David out for some ice cream?"

"On the motorcycle?" David asked in excitement.

"Honey, the day you see me riding that motorcycle is the day I sprout wings. Not the motorcycle. But the ice cream will taste just as good if we go by car."

David grinned. "Yeah. Thanks."

Rachel was grateful that Elizabeth and Jordan were so kind to David, but she was still uncomfortable alone with John.

Rachel silently washed the dishes, acutely aware of John's quiet presence beside her as he dried them. He wore a grim expression around his eyes. She knew how much the loss of his farm was haunting him. That house and land meant everything to John McClennon, who had had very little but those things when he was a boy.

When she finished the last dish, he was leaning on the counter, staring off into space.

"John," she said, gently putting her hand on one of his, "I'm sorry about the farm. I know how much that house meant to you."

He turned his hand over and laced his fingers with hers, then spoke without looking at her. "It was only a house. It can be rebuilt. My family is safe. That's what's important."

"Losing loved ones... That's the worst thing that can happen," she confirmed in a small voice.

"Rachel." He said her name quietly as he turned and pulled her to him. "It was so hard when you left me. I didn't think things would ever be right again."

"And are they?" she asked softly, her voice catching. She wanted so desperately for there to be peace between them. More than that, she wanted him to care again, but she knew she was asking for too much. "Do you still hate me, John?"

He didn't answer her question directly. "I have my farm—or what's left of it," he said with a wry twist of the lips. "And you have your son. I suppose we each have what we need. I've let my anger consume me for too long. There's no point in it now."

Rachel's heart sank. She needed more. She needed him. She hadn't known it until she came back here, but John McClennon would always be a part of her life. She bore a hollow ache in his absence, an ache that grew when she realized that he didn't want her now.

"You should talk to your son's father," John said, and Rachel felt her heart hammer against her ribs. She could feel his own beating steadily beneath her cheek on his chest. "He doesn't know it, but he needs his son in his life. He'll blame you when he realizes it. I don't think I could forgive someone who kept my child from me."

"I... know that." She was near tears. John would never forgive her. What she had done before was a mistake, but this—keeping John McClennon's son from him—was unspeakable.

She couldn't find the courage to tell him. She wasn't ready yet to endure his censure. She felt cowardly and guilty, but she needed him so badly that she couldn't say the one thing that would seal his anger against her forever.

Rachel stood stiffly as John pressed her tightly against his chest. They stood that way a long time before she found her body relaxing against his of its own volition.

"Rachel," he said softly against her hair. "My beautiful Rachel. I've never stopped wanting you."

It almost broke her heart to hear the words. They were so close to what she wanted, to what she could never have.

But she couldn't keep her body from responding to his words. He might not love her, but she was incapable of denying the physical bond that existed between them. They had always had that at least.

Rachel shivered as John's mouth began to move over her face and neck. Her response was instantaneous, nerve endings flickering to life and craving more of his touch. She groaned softly and flexed her hands against his chest, her palms skimming over the fabric of his black T-shirt, eager for the feel of flesh beneath.

John's hands slid to her breasts, teasing them with light caresses through her blouse until her nipples hardened and her knees nearly buckled under the onslaught of sensation.

Rachel's hands traced his shoulders as John lowered his mouth and gently sucked her breasts through her thin blouse. She gasped and clung to him, starving for more of his ministrations.

"John," she groaned as his fingers unbuttoned her blouse even as he continued his maddening caresses. "John, what if David..."

"Don't worry," he soothed her, the blouse now open to his hand. "The ice-cream shop is on the far side of town, and the service is slow. We have lots of time."

For good measure he pulled himself away from her long enough to lock the door, swearing softly as he bumped his shin trying to get back to her quickly through the maze of his furniture. She laughed shakily at that, making his stomach quiver at the sound.

He hadn't given her much reason to laugh lately, and that weighed on him. It wasn't right to punish her for something that had happened when they were both young and foolish.

Not that he wasn't still foolish when it came to Rachel, he reminded himself. All it took was a look from her, one aching look, and he was like some lovesick kid, ready to do anything to be able to touch her.

He made himself stop in front of her so he could enjoy the sight of her blouse wide open to show the lacy pink bra underneath. She flushed but stood still under his gaze.

"I don't think you know how beautiful you are," he murmured, "how much you affect me."

She had never thought herself more than passably attractive, but she did know how she affected him. It was there in his eyes and his face, that handsome face that usually concealed his emotions. There was frank admiration there, and lust as well.

Rachel smiled, almost giddy with her power. "Come on then," she whispered softly. "I don't want to waste a single minute we have alone."

John wondered briefly how often her son's father had seen that seductive smile and been welcomed into her arms. But he refused to let himself dwell on that now. At this moment she stood in front of him, more enticing than he ever remembered her, even in his dreams, and he wasn't going to torment himself with useless questions.

His breathing was shaky as he slid the blouse from her shoulders and reached behind her to unclasp her bra.

When she stood before him in only her jeans, he bent his head and caressed her breasts with his tongue and fingers, unable to get enough of the feel and taste of her. She still smelled as he remembered, the faint scent of lilacs from the sachets she kept in her clothes.

Her hands were on his shoulders as she let her head fall back in wanton pleasure. She whimpered with the need to touch him in return and let her hands slide down his chest and insinuate their way underneath his T-shirt.

At the feel of his flat stomach and hard chest, she groaned. She could feel his muscles trembling beneath her touch.

"If I don't do something now," he ground out, "I'm going to take you here, standing up in a room full of furniture."

"The bedroom," she whispered, turning to go, but he caught her hand.

"I need to hold you," he said, scooping her into his arms and carrying her there.

They couldn't stop touching each other, even after he set her down on the bed. She had his shirt pulled up and was wrestling it over his shoulders. He stopped kissing her neck long enough to let her divest him of it completely.

Rachel swallowed hard. The only light came from the living room, but it shadowed the planes and hard edges of his chest, stomach, arms and shoulders. He was such a beautiful man! She never tired of looking at him. And her body went up in flames every time she did.

"John," she groaned, pulling him to her and pressing urgent kisses on his bare skin.

"Yes, baby," he murmured, as if she were speaking to him through her caresses.

She reached down and undid his jeans. John levered himself up on his arms as she tugged his jeans down past his hips along with his underwear. Rolling over, he quickly kicked off his shoes, socks and jeans in a few short, impatient gestures.

He was lying beside her an instant later, one powerful thigh pinning her legs to the bed. His fingers wreaked havoc on her senses as he caressed her breasts even as he lowered his mouth to kiss them.

Rachel was on fire as his mouth traveled between her breasts, pausing only long enough to allow her tongue time to play with each nipple.

It was maddening, a slow, sweet torment that grew more unbearable by the moment.

Rachel slid her hand down his chest to his stomach, needing to touch him, to drive him as crazy as he was driving her. She let her fingers trail back and forth across his flat abdomen, teasing the sprinkling of hairs there until he groaned and increased his suckling.

Her breath coming in short gasps, Rachel brought her hand lower until she cupped and caressed the fullness of his manhood. Her fingers stroked, matching the rhythm of his ministrations to her breasts, and John's breathing became as ragged as hers.

It took all of his willpower to move himself away from her touch, but he wanted to give her more pleasure before he lost control. And if he let her continue touching him like that much longer, he was definitely going to lose control.

Rachel moaned in frustration as his body slid lower. The moan became a gasp as his mouth turned its sensual attentions to her thighs and the soft flesh between. Her hand grasped his hair, and she writhed beneath him.

"John," she groaned. "Oh, John, please. I can't...take any more. Please."

"I can't, either, sweetheart," he whispered hoarsely, giving her one final intimate kiss there that nearly sent her over the edge.

Rachel began coughing, and John stroked her hair, soothing her until she quieted. He waited, worried that she was too ill, but she urged him on.

John reached for his jeans on the floor and extracted a foil packet from his wallet. He briefly regretted the need to put it on. At one time he would have liked to give Rachel a child. But that gift had come from another man.

Forsaking useless dreams, he brought his body back up to hover over her. Propped on his arms, he looked into her eyes and saw the raw desire he knew was on his own face.

"John," she murmured, almost distraught, and her voice brought him to a halt.

"What is it, Rachel? Tell me."

"Don't regret this, John. Not this time. Please."

"Why would—"

"You regretted it the day we made love in the cabin," she said, interrupting him, not wanting to say this but needing to have it said. "You were so...angry with me afterward. And you've been indifferent since. Please don't feel that way again."

John shook his head, feeling bitter self-reproach for what he'd put her through. He hadn't meant to hurt her. He had only meant to put distance between them.

"Indifferent?" he repeated on a groan. "Rachel, if there's something I've never been toward you it's indifferent. But I haven't been good to you or for you, and I'm sorry for that."

"Don't be sorry," she protested, her fingers shaking as they traced his mouth to silence him. "Just don't...shut me out like that."

"No," he promised. "Not again."

His hands stirred her body back to a fever pitch of arousal, his mouth covering her soft whimpers of pleasure. Her body rose against his, and John entered her then, both of them arching as nerves tautened at the sudden, piercing pleasure.

John drove her slowly toward the heights, his own body crying for release from the tension. She was so soft, so warm and caressing around him that he was a willing prisoner of her flesh. But he wanted to give her pleasure, give her as much as she could stand.

It wasn't until she dug her fingers into his shoulders, her breath only sharp gasps of air against his neck, that he drove into her with a power he couldn't control. Then she was as lost as he, and a moment later the pleasure became almost unbearable until it shattered, leaving them both spent.

She was exhausted and sated and fell asleep with her arm flung over John's chest.

Rachel awoke a short while later to feathery kisses on her spine. She sighed and curled her fingers against the pillow. She was on her stomach, and she was as completely happy as she could remember being in a long time.

"Don't stop," she said huskily when the kisses ended.

"Don't stop?" he teased her. "Not when your son should be home any minute?"

Rachel's eyes flew open, and she sat up quickly. "Oh! Oh, dear. David. Oh, my gosh!" She was struggling to pull on her blouse and jeans, underwear be damned.

John laughed. "Well, maybe any minute was a bit of an exaggeration. We probably have half an hour yet."

"We do?" She eyed him suspiciously, her fingers still on her zipper.

"Possibly."

"Possibly?" Rachel glared at him. "John McClennon, you stop teasing me this instant!"

John laughed again and leaned over to cup her face for a long, intense kiss. "You were only asleep a few minutes," he whispered lazily when he raised his head. "We have time."

"Time for what?" she asked innocently, intent on teasing him this time.

John grinned. "Time for me to wipe that smirk off your face."

"So you think you can, do you?" She smiled in turn.

"Oh, yes, indeed," he said softly. "I'm pretty sure I can."

"And that grin on your face?" she asked teasingly, leaning into his kiss nevertheless.

"I'm sure I'll never get that off my face," he whispered before his mouth claimed hers.

She was lost in the next instant, lost in a hunger that was never completely satisfied. She didn't imagine that it ever would be sated. Her senses dragged in everything that was John, his scent, the feel and taste of his skin, the sound of his heartbeat hammering in his chest, pounding so hard because of her.

Rachel was ready for him almost immediately and urged him to come to her.

As he entered her, she moaned slightly, and John stopped. "Rachel?" he said raggedly. "Are you hurt?"

"Just a little sore, John," she assured him with a shaky smile. "It's been a long time for me. And we were... enthusiastic the last time."

"I'm sorry, sweetheart," he said gently. "I don't want to hurt you."

But nothing would hurt more than if he left her now, caught in this web of desire, her senses clamoring for release.

"Go on, John," she urged him. "Please. I want you too much to stop."

"I want you so much, too," he groaned. But he moved slowly and carefully, treating her so gently that it nearly drove her mad with longing.

John made love to her with iron control, driven by the need not to hurt her, and they were both groaning in frustration as the pleasure grew and sang in their blood and became almost unbearable. When release came, he held himself still inside her, and it was his concern for her that brought her over the edge, panting and clinging to him.

They lay entwined for several minutes, intimately touching, their skin damp and warm. John stroked her face, thinking that he could make love to her again with the briefest of respites. She was a fever in his blood. He could never get enough of her.

"We'd better get dressed," he said at last, regretfully.

She didn't speak, but dressed slowly and without looking at him.

"What's wrong?" John asked as he watched her. "Rachel?" He bent his head to see her face, surprised to see tears in her eyes. "Did I hurt you?" he asked anxiously.

Rachel shook her head. "No, no. I'm fine. It's just..."

But there was no way to explain it to him. She had lied to him and kept his son from him. And now, in the face of his tenderness, she realized what she had forfeited—what she was forfeiting in the future—with that lie.

John would not forgive her again. It was miracle enough that he seemed to have forgiven her for leaving him. His son would be another matter altogether.

"It's been a strain, the flood and everything," he said, rubbing her shoulders. "And you're still exhausted."

Rachel nodded, willing to let him believe her sadness was due to stress. She sat very still, not moving as he stroked her hair and her back and murmured soothing words. She took so much pleasure in his touch, but it was a guilty pleasure.

John groaned at last and levered himself to his feet. "I have to stop, Rachel," he told her. "If I keep touching you like this, I'll make love to you all over again, and you'll be more sore than you already are."

She had to smile at that, and he took her hand, leading her back to the living room.

It wasn't long after they were settled on the couch that they saw headlights approaching the cabin, but it was Norma Curtis who knocked on the door.

She briefly hugged Rachel, assessing her with worried eyes. "I heard that you were sick."

"Word travels fast," Rachel said in surprise.

"You've forgotten how Pierce is," Norma said, laughing. "You can't walk into the clinic or the coffee shop or the beauty shop without someone spreading the word. How are you doing?"

"I'm much better," Rachel assured her.

Norma turned to John. "I'm sorry about your farm," she said, sobering. "I know what a loss it is."

"We did what we could," John said. "Is your house okay?"

"At the moment we're out of danger," Norma replied. "Because of the other levee breaks."

They fell silent as the implications of one farmer's misery being another's salvation hung in the air.

"That's the way it goes," John said at last, and there was no bitterness in his voice.

"Ed Marquist lost his house too," Norma informed them. "I just heard when I was in the grocery store."

John shook his head. "Damn. Ed had a rough couple of years the last three. He had a bad corn crop and then his daughter got sick. The medical bills ate up all the profits from his cattle."

"I hope the government's emergency relief program can help him," Norma said worriedly. "I was hearing about it on the radio today."

John snorted. "A man like Ed won't even apply for relief. You know how most farmers are around here."

Norma nodded. "It'll be tough to give away money if people think it's government charity. And that's not even taking into consideration the red tape. It'll be harvesttime before anyone gets money for seed."

"I could help," Rachel interrupted, and Norma and John turned to look at her.

"How?" Norma asked.

"I know how the government works. Heaven knows, I've had enough experience with their forms. I can help sort through the paperwork and deal with government representatives. I can make sure the money gets to the people who need it in time. And I can advise the farmers on investments so they can have some hedge against a bad year."

She gained enthusiasm as she talked, and Norma and John exchanged glances.

"Rachel could be a big help," Norma acknowledged. "A lot of people will be pretty intimidated when it comes to dealing with a government relief agency."

"Are you sure you're staying here for the long haul?" John asked quietly. "This isn't another whim, is it, Rachel?"

The question stung, but she lifted her chin. Given what had happened before, she knew he had to ask. "I'll stay," she assured him. "I need to do this, John, for me as well as them. I'll waive my fee when it comes to unraveling red tape. They won't be beholden to me in any way."

"They'd listen to you, because you're one of us," John said slowly, and that warmed her more than anything else he could have said. "But they'll want to pay you back, Rachel, in some way."

She shrugged. "We'll work something out if they feel the need."

"Rachel, thank you," Norma said, hugging her. "I've got to go, but I'll spread the word."

When Norma had gone, John stood watching Rachel. "Rachel," he said softly, "what you're doing means a lot to me. These are my friends you're helping. But don't do it because you think you have to redeem yourself somehow. I told you, what's past is past."

But she *was* in need of redemption, she thought. And John would be the last to grant it to her when he found out about his son. *Dear God, why haven't I told him?*

She already knew the answer to that. Because she couldn't bear his anger and coldness. And she would have to live with those things for the rest of her life when he found out what she had done.

She might have told him that she was in need of redemption, but David came barreling through the door the next instant, full of excited chatter about the ice-cream parlor and the drive back past the school.

"Mom!" he cried. "They play soccer here! Jordan told me so!" Then a new worry assailed him. "Gosh, do you think I'm good enough to make the team?"

"I'm sure you are," she assured him, her hand smoothing his hair. But her eyes were on John.

Another good night's sleep combined with the medicine, and Rachel was feeling much better the next morning. She watched John as he cleared the breakfast dishes, talking easily with David.

They were so alike, she thought. Her strong, dark, gentle men.

She allowed herself to think possessively of John because she wanted every luxury of the heart she could get. She had memorized each caress he had given her the day before, each kiss and each moment of lovemaking. She intended the memories to last her a lifetime.

"You need to enlarge the cabin if you and David are going to live here," John said to her from behind the counter.

She looked up from the last of her coffee to watch him studying the outside wall.

"We could knock out this wall and expand over this way. Make your kitchen into an island and put two more bedrooms back here, a bath in between."

"We?" she asked.

"Jake and I. He's been doing renovations. This would be a snap for him."

Rachel sat and considered the proposal. Yes, that would make the cabin more livable and give some much-needed privacy for both her and David.

"John," she said, worry taking over her pleasure. "How much will this cost? I won't feel comfortable financially until I get back to work and have some income."

"We'll work something out," he said, dismissing her worry.

"I can't exactly pay you in chickens or goats," she told him.

"And I told you we'll work it out," he insisted. He turned to David before she could object anymore.

"Want to help me work on the roof today?" he asked.

David's eyes widened. "Really?"

"Sure thing. I have work to do in the attic, and I need your help."

Rachel wouldn't have sent her son into an attic with just anybody, but this was John, and she knew he would take care of David.

"You two be careful," she warned them when they mounted a stepladder and climbed through the opening in the bedroom. "And don't get dirty."

John snorted, and Rachel caught the grin he flashed to David. All right. So she could rule out not getting dirty.

She didn't have time to worry much longer about their state of cleanliness, because Tiny arrived fifteen minutes later with government paperwork.

"I'm sorry to bother you, Rachel," he said, taking off his cap and toeing the floor. "But Norma said you might be able to help me out with this. I ain't never seen the government so damn quick with anything in my life." He shrugged. "It's some federal relief bunch, and they're already set up in town. They're telling everyone to come make their claims." He sank down in the kitchen chair she indicated. "Hell, I don't want to make no claims. But...I got to. Lisa, she's kind of used up all my savings this past year. And I got nothing to rebuild with."

"Let's have a look," Rachel said, gently taking the papers from him. "We'll see what's what."

She worked with Tiny at the table, going over his records and the government forms, one half of her listening to John and David talk in the attic above. Their voices echoed in the small, hollow area, carrying down distinctly to her.

"Is this how you hit a nail, John?" David asked earnestly. The question was followed by a loud thunk.

"Good job," John praised him. "I bet you've used a hammer before."

Rachel could picture David beaming in pride.

"Sometimes I do little things at home, like holding the pipe wrench for Mom."

"You're a handy man to have around," John told him. "You be sure you help your mom now that you're going to live here."

"I will," David said. "You'll be here, too, won't you, John? I mean, we're friends, aren't we?"

"The best of friends," John assured him.

Rachel's heart clenched. The day would come when they would both know the truth. The day that man and boy would know the full extent of what she had done. And that might bring an end to the friendship.

How could she have been so naive? she wondered. She had thought that she was telling John the lie to save his marriage, to save him from certain destruction. Yet, all she'd done was postpone it.

John would be furious. Her son would be wounded.

Someone would have to pay for the lie, and she knew that she would be the one.

"Hey," Tiny said beside her. "Hey, Rachel, you okay?"

Rachel ducked her head and nodded, surreptitiously massaging her temples.

"Just a little headache from my cold," she said. "I'm not quite over it."

She didn't know if Tiny believed her or not, but she bent back to his paperwork, trying hard not to listen to the conversation in the attic.

Ten

The next day dawned clear and still. John and David were working on the roof, taking longer than necessary, Rachel suspected, because of David's "help."

But John had been nothing if not patient and indulgent, and David's pride knew no bounds.

Rachel had been visited by two more farmers concerned about the federal relief paperwork. Actually, they were more concerned that they were taking charity, and Norma had strongly insisted that they discuss that with Rachel.

Rachel had her work cut out for her, but finally she felt that she had gotten through to them, that they understood that the relief aid was rightfully theirs and that they would need help to rebuild.

She had just propped her feet up on the chair opposite hers at the kitchen table and was enjoying a plate of Elizabeth's chocolate-chip cookies when John and David came in from outside. John was finishing the roof work. He hadn't let David climb onto the roof with him, but he kept the boy busy fetching tools and shingles.

"Are you finally alone?" John asked, going to the sink and washing his hands.

"Finally," Rachel echoed. "You farmers sure are a stubborn lot."

John grinned and winked at David, who stood washing his hands beside him.

"You bankers think you run the world," he countered. "We farmers know better."

Rachel tried not to smile as she saw him elbow David, who giggled.

"You farmers wouldn't have machinery or seeds without us bankers," she told him. She watched him walk toward her, and her heart lurched with the self-confident, easy way he did everything. Just like their son.

"And you bankers," he said, reaching around her to snatch one of her precious cookies, "wouldn't have cookies without us farmers growing your flour."

"At least you're not taking credit for chocolate," she grumbled, still trying not to smile. "That would be too presumptuous, even for you, McClennon."

John laughed and sat down beside her. "What do you say," he began, including David in the discussion, "we take the boat out today?"

"Really?" David asked enthusiastically. "Where?"

"The current's slowed down now, and I need to go to the house. Mom had some things on the second floor. If the water rises higher, we won't be able to get to them."

Rachel's heart sank as she remembered how much John had lost in the levee break. She wasn't sure if she could bear to see the house the way it was now.

"Come on, Rachel," John said now. "It'll be fine." He reached over to touch her hand, and she thought how typical it was that he was the one comforting her when it was he who had suffered the loss.

"All right," she said. "I'll go if I can take my cookies."

Rachel had to force herself to keep her eyes on the farmhouse as they approached in the boat. The water reached almost to the second story, and there were marks where the wind had whipped it higher. Only an occasional shingle protruding from the water indicated the roof of the first-story porch. Two of the second-floor windows were broken from the waves, giving the house an old, toothless appearance.

David fell silent, and Rachel clutched his hand. John hadn't looked at them since the house came into view. He sat ramrod straight, eyes unblinking as he throttled down the motor and eased the boat closer.

A lone piece of siding floated past, and Rachel reflexively squeezed David's hand.

When they drew even with the second-story window, John shut off the motor and pulled away broken glass. When most of it was cleared, he reached inside, popped the latch and raised the window frame. With a terse order for them to stay in the boat, he disappeared inside the house, dragging the boat's line with him.

The boat secured, he reached out the window and took David's hand. David's life jacket momentarily caught on the window frame, and then he was inside.

John leaned out to help Rachel. She kept her eyes on his face, not looking down at the dirty water as he levered her inside.

They had entered through John's bedroom window, and Rachel flushed, remembering George's expression when he'd found her in John's bed. Averting her eyes from John's, she followed him toward the door.

"Be careful," he said, his voice devoid of emotion. "The hall's slippery."

Rachel had expected some wetness, but she wasn't prepared for the slime covering the hall at the top of the stairs. She moved David to her side away from the stairs and rested her hand on his shoulder. Daring a glance at the stairs, she saw filthy brown water lapping at the top step. All manner of debris, dead weeds, wood and plastic floated on top.

But the hall was the worst. The water must have washed across it during the high winds, and it left behind dark mud and rotting refuse. A distinct dead-fish smell hung in the air.

Following John, Rachel carefully picked her way down the hall, David sticking close to her side. At least the water hadn't reached the door at the end.

"Wait," John said, stopping in front of the large storage closet. "Let me check first."

Rachel stood back, her arm around David's shoulders, wondering what there was to check for. It definitely worried her.

"Snakes," John explained after poking around the closet with the end of a broom handle. "They get carried away in the flood and look for a high, dry place. When the waters recede, people will find them in their attics mostly."

"Great," Rachel muttered.

"Wow," David said beside her, his eyes wide.

John began pulling boxes from the closet. "Check this, will you?" he asked Rachel, pushing a box toward her with his foot. "I'm looking for Mom's wedding dress."

Rachel hesitated. "Do snakes like to crawl in boxes?"

"Here." He handed her the broom. "Poke around in it with this first."

After much poking to assure herself that nothing slimy was hidden in the box, Rachel pulled away the tissue paper and found the ivory lace beneath. "This is it," she confirmed.

"Good." John was checking other boxes. "Hey, look at this," he said from his squatting position, rocking back on his heels.

Rachel scooted over to look past his shoulder. His fingers were tracing the long, golden hair of a doll.

"Oh." It was all she could say as memory washed over her. John's mother had given her that doll, and Rachel had loved it with every fiber of her being.

"You left it here," John said, stating the obvious.

"I couldn't take it home," Rachel said softly. She looked at John and met his eyes. "My mother—sometimes she got angry at me and broke things when she'd been drinking."

"Was that yours when you were a little kid?" David asked.

"Yes. It was very dear to me."

"Take it," John said, putting the doll into her arms. "Maybe someday...you'll have a little girl who'll play with it the way you did."

Rachel looked away from the anguish in his eyes. She knew he was thinking the same thing she was—they might have had a little girl together if not for her leaving him so long ago.

"Is this yours?" David asked John, reverently touching the old baseball glove that had been under the doll.

John grinned and shook his head. "No, son, that was your mother's, too."

"Mom?" David said in disbelief. "You played baseball?"

"As often as John and his brothers would let me play with them," she assured him. "Here," she said, handing the glove to David. "I guess this should be yours now."

David sat on a relatively clean piece of hall carpet and looked at the glove in his lap.

"You going to try it on for fit?" John asked him.

"No, sir," David said, then, "I mean, yes, sir. I guess what I mean is I've never played baseball. Everybody in my apartment plays soccer."

John's eyebrows went up. "I guess we'll have to remedy that then, won't we?"

David dared a small look at him. "You mean you'd play with me?"

"And your mother," John said, trying not to smile. "But you've got to watch her. She argues with the ump."

David grinned, and Rachel punched John's arm.

"Hey, look, there's more in there," David said, rooting through the box and coming up with a photo album. "Mom, is this you as a kid?"

Rachel looked over his shoulder and grimaced. The photo of a very skinny, straight-haired urchin smiled back at her. "Ugh," she said. "I look like one of those pathetic children in need of a sponsor."

"Not so pathetic," John said as he lifted his mother's portable sewing machine from the closet and started for the boat. "That was your birthday. Eleventh, I think. Mom made you a cake, and I let you ride the tractor with me. I bet you don't even remember."

He went on to the boat, Rachel's eyes following him. She remembered it, but she hadn't thought he would. She could still recall the perfect happiness of that day, partially because it was a birthday unmarred by her mother's errant habits. But mostly because she had ridden the tractor behind John.

"Look at this," David said, pulling a small box out and opening it. Inside was a ring, a small amethyst.

"My birthstone ring," Rachel said, her voice faltering. John had given it to her for her sixteenth birthday. And she had given it back the night she left town for good. She felt something akin to physical pain when she picked up the ring. Her hand was shaking.

Gently she closed the box and put it back with the other things. "Come on, David," she said. "Let's carry these photo albums for John."

She gathered them up and stood, finding John standing behind her when she turned around. He wasn't looking at her, though. His eyes were on the box with the ring.

Rachel couldn't take her eyes off his face, mesmerized by the raw emotion there, the pain and the loneliness. John wouldn't look at her.

Rachel hesitated, then moved on down the hall after David. It was over now, she told herself. John had said it himself. The past was in the past. But she blinked back sudden tears as she realized the power the past had to hurt her.

"This *thing* between you and John," David said in a low voice at the window. "It goes back a long way, doesn't it?"

Rachel had laid the albums in the boat, and now she straightened and faced her son. "I already told you that John and I were very good friends, one time."

"Mom, you don't have to talk around stuff with me. Honest. I can understand. You were in love, weren't you?"

"I . . . yes, we were."

"And you still love him, don't you?" David persisted.

"David, I . . ." But she couldn't go on with any more lies. She had already piled one on top of another until she was caught in a web of deceit that threatened to destroy her. She had enough of lying, enough of "protecting" John and David from the truth.

"Yes," she said simply, aware of John standing just inside the door. "Yes, I still love him."

She abruptly turned and started to leave the room. She had to squeeze past John in the doorway, and he reached out as if to stop her, then let his hand fall away. Afraid of what she might see in his face, Rachel couldn't look at him. She went on to the hall and bent down to pick up the doll. She felt tears again and knelt, holding the doll to her as if it gave some comfort from the past.

They continued loading the boat then without speaking, and when John helped Rachel climb out the window, his hands didn't linger. He released her as soon as she had her balance and turned to the task of casting off.

She had no idea what he was thinking since hearing her admission, but she felt miserable as she imagined the worst. And still ahead of her lay the dreaded task of telling him the whole truth.

John talked to David on the trip back, and Rachel sat silently, listening to them and wishing she had never lied to John about her pregnancy. Things would be so much simpler now.

And yet she couldn't honestly say she would do things differently given the choice again. She had detested the way her mother lived her life, the way she bedded any man who wanted her, married or not. She knew she could never have forced herself to jeopardize John's marriage to Meredith by telling him about his son. She could hold her head up, knowing she'd had no hand in the end of John's marriage.

But she may have sacrificed her own chances of happiness with John along the way. Suddenly she felt as tired as she had before she'd begun recovering from the bronchitis.

Jordan and Jake helped them unload things at Elizabeth's apartment. Mason was sleeping in the back bedroom, and Elizabeth told them that he'd been feeling miserable since his drinking bout and to let him rest.

Jordan paused by John when they reached the truck. "I'm leaving for home tonight," he said. "I've been away from the office long enough. Time to get back to work."

John clapped him on the shoulder. "Thanks. I've appreciated the help."

"I'm sorry we couldn't save the house," Jordan said, shaking his head. "Jake and I have a lot of childhood memories that washed away with the flood, but you—it was your home."

John shrugged. "I'll rebuild."

Rachel slid a box from the truck and went back to the apartment. She hated seeing this stoicism in John, this refusal to acknowledge the pain. It was as if he were determined not to let anything hurt him again.

"I'm sure grateful that you live on the first floor, Mom," Jake said as he set the sewing machine on the living room carpet. "After sharing a bed with Mason last night and listening to Jordan snore out here on the couch, I don't think I could handle anything vertical."

Elizabeth smiled. "Jordan's leaving tomorrow, so you won't have to put up with the sleeping arrangements past tonight."

"I wasn't complaining," he said, pressing a kiss onto the top of her head. "Oh, hell, yes, I was. I'm going to have to leave soon myself. They say the water's finally starting to go down."

"If it doesn't rain any more, it might keep dropping," Elizabeth said. "I'm glad you came. John needed you both here."

Jake nodded, frowning. "It's been hard on him, losing the house. And the crop this year, maybe most of next year's. But it's like there's something else on his mind. I don't know." Jake shrugged. "Maybe I'm imagining things. Sometimes I think I see things too clearly since I stopped drinking."

Rachel edged toward the door, embarrassed to be eavesdropping, but understanding what Jake meant. She had seen the same sadness in John, even before the flood took the house.

John and Jordan came in then, David trailing after them, and the conversation turned to Jordan's morning departure.

"You know these big business tycoons," Jake said, winking at John. "He has a ton of work waiting for him."

"And probably an impatient woman or two," John said dryly.

Jordan grinned. "Gentlemen, I never divulge secrets, industrial or otherwise."

Jake snorted. "He's as cocky as he was as a kid," he said to John. "I told you twenty-five years ago we should have traded him for an autographed baseball when we had the chance."

"Ah, if only we'd had the foresight," John said. Crossing his arms, he glanced at David. "What do you say we all go out and have some fun tonight? Maybe take David to the carnival down at the Bison grounds."

"The Bison grounds?" David repeated curiously.

"It's a local fraternal organization," Rachel told him. "A men's club."

"They're having their annual picnic," John said. "You think you want to go, David?"

David was enthusiastic. Rachel thought it was an all-male night out until John grabbed her hand.

"Come on, Rachel," he said. "You can show off your pitching arm for David at the games."

He let go of her hand almost immediately, and she felt bereft. She followed the men out the door, wishing desperately for time alone with John to talk.

Elizabeth declined the offer to accompany them, and Rachel found herself wedged in the front seat of John's truck, between him and Jake. Jordan and David were in the seat behind them.

She was pressed close to John, but he seemed not to notice. His indifference was worse for her than it had been after the first time they'd made love. Now he knew that she loved him.

John was silent despite Jake's attempts at conversation, and finally Jake looked sideways at Rachel and shrugged.

Rachel remembered that years ago when she would come to the Bison picnic she would leave at dark because of the rough crowd that gathered in the shadows of the carnival, drinking and laughing loudly. But it wasn't dark yet today, and though the rides were in motion this was a far more benign atmosphere than she remembered.

She hadn't had any lunch yet, and John steered her and David toward the food stands. Jordan and Jake went off by themselves, leaving Rachel to feel uncomfortable in John's presence. He still was studiously avoiding looking at her.

They sat at a picnic table in the shade with grilled Polish sausage sandwiches and lemonades. David was busily planning what he would ride and in which order, and Rachel was half listening. John sat across from her, his face as unreadable as in the truck.

David finished first, and Rachel let him go to the Ferris wheel alone. She could see it from where she sat. There were already four children on it, laughing and squealing as it carried them up and around.

"John," Rachel said without looking at him, "we need to talk."

"Yes," he said, and she could feel his eyes on her. "But not here."

"I don't care where," she said impatiently. "I just know that I'm going to scream if you don't tell me what's wrong."

"Tell you what's wrong?"

At the surprise in his voice, she did look at him. His blue eyes were boring into her with an intensity that would have made her shiver except for the sticky warmth of the air surrounding them.

"You've been so...detached," she began, stumbling over the words now that she was looking into his face. "At the house, then at your mother's and now here. As though nothing else exists. Even Jake noticed it."

"That's hardly cause for worry," he said wryly.

"But it is, John. I'm afraid..." She didn't want to tell him what she feared—that he was deliberately shutting her out because he didn't want her loving him.

"Afraid of what, Rachel?" he asked softly.

Afraid of living my life without you. Afraid you'll reject your son. Afraid to love you.

She plunged in against her better judgment. "I'm afraid you're not letting yourself feel anything because of the flood, because of what you lost."

"What I lost," he repeated quietly, his eyes leaving hers to focus on something intangible in the distance. "But there's compensation for houses, isn't there, Rachel? Is there a government agency to compensate me for losing you?"

When she didn't answer, he said, "Eleven years, Rachel. Eleven long years. We've wasted them, you and I. Where's the compensation for that?"

She almost said it. *Your son.* But she couldn't. Not here with the crowd milling around. And not when he hadn't told her how he felt about her.

They stared at each other in silence until they realized that someone was calling John's name. Rachel looked up to see Meredith hurrying across the straw path between the rides, holding on to the sun hat on her head. She was wearing shorts, a stretch top and sandals, and the carnival workers were watching her with interest.

"I'm so glad I ran into you," she said brightly to John when she reached the picnic table. "I really need your help. My hot-water heater's not working."

"What about your landlord?" John asked wearily. "Can't he fix it?"

Meredith made a face. "You know how he is. If he comes to my apartment, I'll never get rid of him."

Which was what Meredith would like to see happen with John, Rachel suspected.

"I have to wash my hair tonight," Meredith pleaded. "And I don't have any clean dishes even."

John sighed and levered himself up from the table. "All right. Rachel, can you and David ride home with Jake and Jordan?"

Rachel nodded, and Meredith sent a bright smile in her direction. "Thanks so much."

John gave her the keys to his truck and assured her that Meredith would give him a ride home.

Rachel watched them walk away, Meredith talking animatedly, then sighed and went to join David.

Jake dropped her off at Elizabeth's apartment later, then took David to help Jordan wash his car before his trip home the next day.

Rachel sat in the upholstered chair in Elizabeth's living room, not bothering to brush away the hair that had blown across her face during the truck ride here. She was tired and discouraged, and she despaired of John ever loving her again.

"Where is everybody?" Elizabeth asked when she came in with a bag of groceries.

Rachel told her, trying not to sound so aggrieved about Meredith appropriating John.

Elizabeth laughed. "That girl is always dragging him off to fix something or other."

"I know what it is she really wants him to fix," Rachel said, then immediately regretted her words. "I'm sorry. That was catty."

"No, honey, it was true," Elizabeth said, setting down the groceries and patting Rachel's shoulder.

Together they put the groceries away in the kitchen.

"Meredith always wanted John," Elizabeth said. "She knew he was in love with you, and I guess she decided that she could settle for him not loving her. I think she found out that that's not a happy way to live a marriage."

"John wouldn't marry someone he didn't love," Rachel said, putting the coffee in the cupboard.

"Honey, he had a broken heart, and I don't think he knew what he was feeling. Meredith took advantage of that."

Rachel's hands stilled, and she slowly turned around. Sighing, she sagged back against the counter. "I hurt him badly, Elizabeth, and I never meant to."

"I know," Elizabeth said with a sad smile. "But I think you've both suffered enough for that. You're both older now, and you know what's important. You could have a fine life together. John's grown quite fond of David in the short time he's been here. We all have."

"Oh, Elizabeth," Rachel groaned, lowering her head to her hands. "That's just it. John will never forgive me for what I've done. When he finds out, I'll never see him again."

"When he finds out about what?" Elizabeth asked with some alarm. "Rachel, what is it you've done?"

"It's David. He's..." She couldn't finish and lowered her hands to face Elizabeth.

"Oh," Elizabeth said as though someone had punched her in the stomach. "Oh." She sat down quickly at the kitchen table, her eyes fixed on Rachel. "John is David's father?" she asked tremulously.

Rachel nodded her head. "I wanted to tell him. I've wanted to tell him so badly."

"But why didn't you?" Elizabeth asked, looking as if she were still in shock.

"When I found out that I was pregnant, I couldn't face him just then, not after the awful things I'd said to him when I left. And then, later, I found out that he was married. I couldn't tell him then. I just couldn't.''

"Oh, you poor child," Elizabeth said, rising and going to put her arms around Rachel. "What you must have gone through." She held Rachel away after a long hug and managed a smile. "But, you know, I'm glad David is John's. He's a wonderful boy, and it will be so nice to have a child around. We all grieved so long when Jake lost his wife and their baby."

Rachel smiled at her through her tears. "It's been so hard with him not knowing and me imagining his reaction. And yet, it's almost harder to make myself tell him. I've put it off so long that it gets worse every day."

Elizabeth gave her another hard squeeze and nodded. "Don't put it off any longer. He has to be told. And though he may be angry at first, I think he'll understand in time."

In time. Rachel's heart ached. She had had enough of time. She longed for John every waking minute. He even invaded her dreams. She couldn't stand to wait on time any longer. She wanted John now.

"A grandson," Elizabeth said, clapping her hands and laughing. "I'm finally a grandmother again."

The sun was already low in the sky when Rachel had asked Jake to drive her and David back to the cabin. John hadn't returned, and she had resolutely forced herself not to imagine him alone with Meredith in her apartment. She had fixed sandwiches, then she and David sat on a small outcropping of rock on the bluff and watched the clouds on the horizon change from scarlet to purple to pink to gray.

She had glanced at her son's profile and thought how much he looked like his father at that age.

John came by the cabin when he was finished at Meredith's, his hands greasy and black, his hair mussed. Rachel watched him wash his hands at her sink, tempted to reach out and brush the dirt from his shirt and jeans but afraid to touch him. It was as if she were made of glass, and if she let him too close to her she would shatter into a million pieces.

He looked tired, but he smiled at her and took David outside to play baseball. He asked Rachel if she wanted to play, too, but she said she was too tired. In truth, she knew that she couldn't concentrate on anything other than John at the moment.

It was dusk when he finally told David he couldn't throw another pitch or chase another fly ball. Rachel heard them laughing as John gathered up the bat and ball and walked slowly toward the cabin. She came outside and sat on the top step, and John lowered himself beside her, stretching out his jeans-clad legs and groaning.

"You've been working too hard," she told him. "All the sandbagging on the levee, the late nights, no sleep. You need some rest."

"See if I listen any better than you did when I tried to get you to rest," he informed her, but not without humor.

They lapsed into silence again, and Rachel could feel her heart hammering against her ribs as she gathered her courage to tell him. David was at the far end of the yard, catching fireflies. *Our son.*

This was how it should be, a man, a woman and their child relaxing peacefully on a summer night. But there was still no peace between her and John.

"I have something to tell you," he said at last, his head lowered to stare at his hands between his knees. "To ask, actually."

"I do, too." She swallowed.

"I need to go first."

If she hadn't been so nervous, she would have smiled. Just like when they were children, and they fought to see who would go first. She glanced sideways at him and saw that he was still concentrating on his hands. He looked so tired and so sad that she wanted to take his hands in hers and just hold them.

"I brought this back with me," he said, and it took her a minute to see what it was that he was turning around in one hand. Her birthstone ring.

"But why?" she asked without thinking. She had practically thrown it at him when they had parted. It had been a gift from him once, and she had returned all his gifts. *Except for his son.*

"I think we've both been miserable long enough," he said. "I don't want to go on like this."

"Like what?" she asked, her throat constricted with need and with dread of what he might say.

"You know. The way we've been to each other. Distant, pretending that all the anger is still there."

"Isn't it, John?" she replied, thinking of how he'd been toward her today. She wanted him so badly, but she didn't want just a part of him. She wanted all of John David McClennon, with nothing held back to satisfy old anger.

"No," he said quietly. "I've been pretending it is, but it's not, Rachel. It's gone. I said that we should leave the past in the past, but I didn't really believe it then. Now I do. It's over. But it's never going to be over between us."

"We can't bury the past in bed, John," she said sadly.

"Rachel, we've been friends from the time we were children. And we've been in love and we've been lovers. I think we'll always be in love no matter what happens to the other two."

Rachel finally looked at him. So afraid of what she'd see. But he'd said they would always be in love. That meant . . .

His eyes were the deepest blue she'd ever seen. But there was pain there, too, and she knew that she'd put it there. And she would have to give him more pain. *His son.*

"John, I—" she began, wanting to end her misery or begin it, all by telling him the truth.

"Take the ring back, Rachel," he said, gently putting it in her palm and closing her fingers around it. "Take it. I need you as a friend and as a lover. I need you in my life."

My friend. Oh, God in heaven, what had she done?

Tears gathered in her eyes. "John, I have to talk to you. I'm not finished with the past, and you aren't, either, even though you don't realize it." It was agony to go on. His face was puzzled and a little hurt, as if he expected her to tell him she didn't love him, that she didn't want him. But she did. She wanted him so much that she was risking everything.

She never got a chance to tell him.

Jake's car pulled into the drive, and he jumped out, shouting. "Have you seen Mason?"

"No," Rachel said, rising, a lump in her throat. She couldn't quite concentrate on what he was saying. She was still intent on what she had to tell John.

"We've got to go find him," John said, and she turned uncomprehending eyes on him. "Come on," he urged. "If he's with Lisa, he's probably been drinking. It might help for him to see you."

She went with him, her steps leaden, her mind still on what she had to say. *John, listen to me, please!*

They dropped David off at Elizabeth's apartment, where Rachel finally dragged her attention to the events at hand and found out what had happened. Lisa had come by the apartment, and it was apparent she had been drinking. Over Elizabeth's objections, Mason left with her.

John and Jake decided to expand the search by splitting up. Jake would take his car and try Mason's favorite taverns in town. John and Rachel would search the outskirts.

As she rode with John away from town, Rachel realized she was still clutching the birthstone ring, and she shoved it into her pocket.

Rachel Tucker and her wayward brother. She shook her head to dispel the image. Mason was charming and outgoing when he wanted to be, but it was a dark charm born of an uncertain childhood. Rachel and Mason had learned what to do to survive, and perhaps it hadn't served either of them very well.

John had been right, she thought. She was the one who tried to fix things, who took care of everyone. Mason was the one who lapsed into irresponsibility, letting the world take care of him as best it would.

John stopped first at a run-down tavern just at the edge of town. He told Rachel to stay in the car while he checked inside. The neon lights blinked on, and Rachel noted absently that about a third of them were burned out.

John came back out quickly, shaking his head at her questioning look. "They haven't seen them today."

They stopped at three more taverns, each more seedy than the last, but still there was no sign of either Lisa or Mason.

Rachel sagged back against the seat as they drove on. Streetlights fluttered on in the gathering darkness, and fireflies drifted over the yards and fields they passed.

She and Mason had never chased fireflies the way David did. It had seemed a frivolous activity for two children who didn't know where their next meal was coming from. Their pleasures were measured in minutes, not days. A day at the carnival was something to treasure for months.

The carnival. That was it.

"I think I know where they are," she said, sitting up straight in the seat. "The carnival."

John turned the truck around and took a gravel road. Minutes later they pulled behind one of the many cars parked on the side of the road. The carnival was in full swing, the bright lights blinking, the rides whirling, the music drifting on the air.

"John," Rachel said, putting her hand on his arm as they started toward a straw-covered path leading through the gate. "What are we going to do if we find him?"

"I don't know. We may not be able to do anything. But at least we're trying."

"John! Rachel!"

They turned and saw Jake running toward them from a parking spot farther down the road.

"A guy at the tavern told me Mason's here," he said when he caught up to them. "Lisa's with him."

"Has he been drinking since he left your mother's place?" Rachel asked hesitantly, not sure if she should confront her brother if he was roaring drunk.

"I don't think so," Jake said. "It sounds like Lisa has been, though."

They walked together through the grounds, Rachel hardly taking notice of the cooking aromas or the shrill cry of the barkers. She felt as if she were on a rescue mission, much the same as when she was a little girl and she had to find Mason because he'd missed too much school. Back then she had somehow searched taverns and alleys on her own; now she wasn't quite so brave. She was grateful for John's and Jake's presence. She felt almost as if she were confronting her own past.

They didn't speak as they passed the food stands and the games and the rides. Rachel knew where they were headed—the shadowy outskirts of the carnival, the dark place under the trees where people congregated to drink beer. They veered off the straw path and trod across grass damp with the evening dew.

She didn't see Mason at first. The lights from the carnival didn't penetrate the trees this far from the last ride, and she nearly tripped over a thick cord that ran to a generator.

John steadied her, and when she looked again at the crowd of men in their jeans and T-shirts, she saw him. He was standing quietly away from the crowd, his eyes intent on someone else.

Lisa Harmon, Rachel realized as her eyes sought to penetrate the gloom. The girl was dressed in a skimpy halter top and cutoff shorts. Her eyes were overly bright, as was her laugh. She took frequent, long sips from a can of beer, and she seemed to be ignoring Mason.

"You okay, man?" Jake asked in a low voice as they drew next to Mason.

He turned to face them, a wry smile on his face, and nodded. Rachel was struck by the sadness on his face. He's too young to look like that, she thought.

"I haven't had anything to drink," Mason said to Jake. "I was trying to keep Lisa from coming here, but you can see what a great success I was."

"You should know better than anyone else that no one can save us from ourselves."

"Yeah. I know."

He might know it, Rachel thought, but he was having a hard time accepting it.

"I see you brought out the heavy artillery," Mason said, giving Rachel a gentle smile.

"Was I ever that rough on you?" she demanded, so relieved that he wasn't drinking that she barely got any levity into the question.

"Like a mother hen with armor," he assured her. "You were the toughest fourteen-year-old in history."

Rachel couldn't smile at that. It was true. She'd been so determined to make a home despite her mother that she'd probably run roughshod over poor Mason.

"I didn't mind, though," he told her, squeezing her shoulder.

"Well, well, the gang's all here," Lisa said noisily, sloshing the can of beer as she took a step toward them. "Afraid I'm going to corrupt him?"

"Stay out of this, Lisa," Mason said.

"Why? So you can run along behind your sister and your friends like a dog with your tail between your legs?"

"You've had too much to drink," Mason said. "I'm going home."

The men standing around had stilled, obviously interested in the conversation. A few hid their smiles. In the darkness they looked almost like extensions of the trees.

Mason turned to go, but Lisa grabbed his arm. "Don't you walk out on me!"

Mason slowly but deliberately pulled her hand from his arm. "Come see me when you're sober."

He walked away, and Rachel turned to follow him, feeling relief wash over her.

"Don't you walk away from me!" Lisa shouted behind them. "None of you has the right to pass judgment on me!"

Rachel didn't realize she was trembling until John put his arm around her shoulders.

"Not even you, Rachel Tucker!" Lisa screamed.

No, Rachel pleaded. *Not here.* The blood was pounding in her head, and it was an effort to put one foot in front of the other.

"You're no better than me," she shouted. "Not when you had John McClennon's bastard!"

John abruptly stopped, and Rachel froze.

"What did you say?" John said as he turned around.

"I said that your friend there had your baby, and she still thinks she's better than me. But you never married her, did you?" Lisa laughed, an ugly sound that made Rachel's skin crawl.

"What is she talking about?" John demanded, his hands coming down on Rachel's shoulders.

The pressure hurt, making her wince. "I tried to tell you," she began.

"Tell me what?" he said, his voice rising. "What is she talking about, Rachel?"

"David," she whispered.

John's hands fell from her shoulders, and a look of utter shock came over his face. "Dear God," he whispered hoarsely. "Are you saying..."

Rachel's eyes dropped from the growing coldness in his. He no longer looked like the man she knew.

"I wanted to tell you," she said, knowing how inadequate that sounded. "I just didn't want to hurt you."

"I think you've done a pretty good job, nevertheless," he said sharply. "Why, Rachel? I wasn't good enough to be your husband, and I wasn't good enough to be your child's father?"

"John, it wasn't—"

But she didn't finish. He was already walking swiftly away into the darkness, his shoulders stiff, his head down.

She was left standing alone, watching his retreating figure and knowing that she had ruined their lives eleven years ago... And she had ruined their lives again tonight.

Eleven

Jake had taken her to the apartment, then driven her and David to the cabin. Rachel didn't even remember what Jake said, but he had said something in an effort to comfort her before awkwardly backing out the door.

Even David had hardly said a word, recognizing that something was wrong.

It was her worst nightmare, the one she had relived the past eleven years. John didn't want anything to do with her.

Rachel sat on the cabin's porch, staring up at the sky. David was in bed, but she hadn't been able to sleep. It must be midnight by now, but the guilt continued to eat at her.

She hadn't wanted to hurt John back then, and she had ended up hurting both of them beyond repair. What bond they had was irrevocably broken.

She shoved her hands into her pockets as the humid air cooled and chilled her. Her fingers touched something hard and round, and with a groan she remembered the ring.

Slowly she tightened her fist around it. John had wanted to marry her. She lowered her head to her knees and cried quietly, her hair sticking to her face as the tears flowed.

She felt someone sit down beside her, and then David's arms were around her shoulders.

"Don't cry, Mom," he whispered shakily. "What's the matter?"

When she regained control of herself, she wiped her face and gave him a tremulous smile.

"I did a really stupid thing, honey," she began. "I kept a big secret because I thought it was best. But it wasn't my decision to make. And now John's angry with me."

"He is? How come? You two are a hot item."

"Not anymore," she said wistfully. She took David's hand in hers and squeezed it. "This secret has something to do with you, too."

"It does? Wow."

Carefully and gently she told David the identity of his father, gingerly skirting the question of why she'd kept the information secret.

His first reaction was a pleased, "Cool!" And then he grew thoughtful. "Do you think John's mad at me, too?" he asked.

"No, honey," she assured him. "I think he's very proud to have you as a son. I'm the one who screwed things up here."

The phone was hooked up now, and Elizabeth called twice to see how Rachel and David were doing. She didn't mention John, and Rachel worked hard not to ask. It had been a week since the disaster at the carnival. Mason had come by to apologize for what Lisa had done, but Rachel held no grudges. What had happened had been her own fault from the beginning.

The floodwater was slowly receding, and each evening Rachel went to stand on the bluff to look down at John's house. It wasn't pretty anymore, looking derelict and abandoned with its broken windows and grimy exterior. It reminded her of her memories, bruised and more the worse for wear.

Rachel stepped to the porch, stopping to drape a rug over the railing before she started for the bluff. When she turned, her heart lurched to her throat. Coming up the path was John, looking impossibly handsome to her lonely eyes. He walked slowly, his back straight, his dark hair mussed and his blue eyes—oh, those sad blue eyes!—looking seemingly past her.

Rachel waited, her hands clutching the railing.

He stopped when he drew opposite her, but his expression didn't change. "Where's David?" he asked.

"He went to collect rocks by the woods." She gestured feebly toward the trees behind the cabin.

"Does he know about me?"

"Yes," she said, meeting his eyes. "He's...very happy about it."

"Why didn't you tell him before?" Again, that accusing note in his voice.

"A faceless father didn't seem much better than no father at all," she said quietly.

"I want the right to see him whenever I choose," he said, his jaw firm. His eyes still showed no emotion, and Rachel wanted to scream at him. *Yell at me! Anything but this indifference!*

"Of course. I wouldn't deny you that."

He started to say something, then seemed to think better of it. "Could I take him now? To go for a ride?"

"Yes. I'll get him."

She came down the steps and started to walk to the side of the cabin, but John caught her arm. "I'd like to get him myself," he said. She acquiesced with a nod of her head, but still he didn't let go of her arm.

"I'll get my furniture out of here as soon as I have a place to put it," he said.

She nodded. "There's no hurry."

"Why did you do it, Rachel?" he demanded suddenly.

She didn't pretend not to understand what he meant.

"I didn't know that I was pregnant for a while, and then when I did I was afraid to tell you."

"But why?"

"Because of the...bad feelings between us when I left."

"Didn't you know that no matter what had happened that I would—" He broke off and shook his head as if to clear it. "No, I suppose you didn't."

"And then I found out that you were married, and I couldn't. There didn't seem to be anything I could do. I was making enough money, and I wanted my baby. I suppose I didn't think about how much you might want him, too."

"No, you didn't." The coldness was back in his voice, making her shiver despite the evening's lingering heat.

"I'm not going to ask you to forgive me for the lie," she said evenly. "I know the pain I've caused, and I'll have to live with that. But what I did was because I cared for you, and I didn't want to take you away from your chance for happiness with Meredith."

She flinched when his fingers tightened on her arm, but more from his expression of utter abhorrence than from the pressure of his touch.

"There was never any other man?" he demanded.

She shook her head.

"I should have known," he said with deceptive calmness. "I knew when I found out you were pregnant that I should go see you, talk to you. But I took the easy way out and phoned."

"It wasn't the easy way out," she assured him. "There was no easy way out for either of us."

Abruptly he dropped his hand and moved away from her, the expression on his face more revealing than she was sure he would have wanted. She saw the longing, and she knew he was feeling the same cruel misery that she was. He looked at her a long time, the old pain in his eyes, before he went behind the house.

Rachel went inside, not wanting to see him again when he left with David. I can't do this, she thought miserably. I can't see him and not want to touch him, to talk to him, to share his bed.

But she had no choice in the matter. She would have to wait for him to decide if he ever wanted her in his life again.

The days grew hotter as the month passed. Rachel planted flowers around the cabin and worked on cross-stitch samplers for the walls. In the evening she would go stand on the bluff and watch John's house.

The water was gone now, leaving in its wake a brown paste over everything. Sometimes in the afternoon the stench rose as high as the bluff.

John was there at the house occasionally, carting out rubble and shoveling muck from the floors. She didn't stand on the bluff when he was there, because she couldn't bear to realize that he was so close and so unattainable.

When he came to get David, he was cordial to her, but she tried to make herself scarce to avoid the awkwardness. She never questioned David about his time with his father, only listened without comment when he felt the need to talk. She could tell that the bond between father and son was deepening. She was glad of that, at least.

She knew from talking to Elizabeth that Jake had gone home and that John was staying at Elizabeth's apartment. John's furniture was still in the cabin, and sometimes she ran her hands over it, thinking of him touching the wood and feeling some comfort in the secondary contact.

She noticed that he seemed to seek her out when he came for David, lingering longer each time. But she wouldn't let herself hope.

It rained three weeks after his first visit with David, and the roof the two of them had worked on together sprang a small leak. "What did John do last time to fix this?" she asked David.

He explained to her about finding the leak and replacing worn shingles and showed her where John had put the materials he'd used. Then he suggested she ask John to do it. They had both seen John working inside his house that morning, but neither had spoken about it.

But Rachel didn't want to bother John. She wasn't going to be like Meredith, using every leaky faucet and squeaky door as an excuse to see him.

She got out the ladder and leaned it against the house with David's help. Then she climbed up with a hammer, the roofing nails and a couple of shingles. The ladder rocked but held its position.

"Mom, you don't even know where the leak is," David protested. "And it's getting windy out here."

"Go inside before you get soaked," she insisted. "I'll only be a minute."

She saw him hesitate, then retreat to the porch. "All right," she muttered to herself. "This shouldn't take long." The hammer in one hand, she scanned the roof and saw two loose shingles. With a triumphant exclamation she inched upward on her knees and as quickly as she could, drove two extra nails in to hold the shingles down. The wind gusted, and she crouched where she was before inching backward to the ladder. "David!" she called. "I'm coming down now."

She found her footing on the ladder and started inching her way down. From the corner of her eye she could see David anxiously waiting on the porch. She was almost halfway down when the wind gusted again, and the ladder shifted. In the next second she realized that she was falling, the ladder with her. David shouted something just before she hit hard on her back.

The next thing she knew he was pulling the ladder off her and bending over her in the rain. She tried to say something, but the wind was knocked out of her and she couldn't get any words out. The look of terror on David's face, if not the bruising ache in every muscle, was enough to make her regret ever climbing the damn ladder.

"Mom! I'll get John!"

David took off running before she could get enough breath back to stop him. *John.* How was she going to face him? Especially when she was lying on her back with rain running into her ears and nose. She remembered stories she'd heard of turkeys drowning themselves by staring up at the sky during a rainstorm. It made her wonder if she was really much brighter than the average turkey.

Slowly she pushed herself to a sitting position and gingerly flexed her muscles, twisting first one way, then the other. Nothing seemed to be broken or sprained, though she knew she would be stiff and sore the next day. Her pride, however, bore grievous harm. She didn't want John to find her sitting in the rain like this, but she just didn't have the energy to move at the moment.

She was about to try standing when John topped the hill at a dead run, David keeping up as best he could. "Rachel!" he called, dropping to one knee beside her. "Are you all right?"

"You're going to get wet," she admonished him.

"I'm already wet," he countered. "Where does it hurt?"

"All over," she told him truthfully. "But I'm all right. I just got the wind knocked out of me."

After assuring himself that she was basically okay, John slipped his arms under her and gathered her into his arms as he stood. He strode into the house while David held the door. Cursing under his breath at his furniture impeding his progress, he maneuvered around chests and chairs to set her down on the couch. He sat beside her and gently cupped her face. David hovered behind John, pacing nervously.

"Are you crazy!" John demanded of her.

His voice was such a sharp contrast to his gentle hands that she nearly laughed. "Yes," she said, sighing. "I'm crazy. There, are you happy?"

"No!" he barked in the same aggrieved voice. "I'm not happy, and it's your fault."

"I know," she said, sighing again. "It's all my fault."

"No, it's not," he said, immediately contradicting her. "It's my own stupid fault for letting you go when I should have gone to you."

"All right, it's your fault." She was too glad to see him to argue about anything. She wanted him to keep touching her like this forever. His hands had left her face and were tenderly stroking her arms and her shoulders.

He looked mildly surprised at her agreement, but he shook his head. "I don't want to think about whose fault anything is. I don't want to think about what happened a long time ago. I don't want to live with this kind of ache anymore."

Her heart clenched. "What *do* you want, John?" she asked softly.

"Isn't it obvious?" he replied dryly. "I can't sleep at night. I can't work. I can't eat."

"Oh, boy," David anxiously whispered as he paced.

"What do you want me to do about it?" Rachel asked.

"I want you to stay away from ladders from now on," he said. "And I don't want you telling any more lies because you think it's best for me."

"Is that all?" she asked, unable to look away from the light in his deep blue eyes.

He shook his head. "I want you to go to a church with me and stand up in front of everybody and say you'll be my wife."

"Why?" she whispered as her heart fluttered wildly. She had to hear him say it.

"Because I love you," he said, finally giving her what she wanted. "Because I've always loved you and I've been miserable without you. Because I love my son, and I want us to finally be a family."

Behind him David dropped to one knee and pumped his arm. "Yes," he said triumphantly. "Yes!"

"John David McClennon," she said quietly, "I have always loved you and I always will."

He smiled then, for the first time in weeks. He could feel his heart swell with emotion, love for Rachel and for their son. He had been lost and alone in the past for a long time, but finally he could move forward with his life. What he had once lost had come full circle, and though his love for Rachel wasn't the love of youth anymore, it was something better. Something richer and deeper.

He closed his eyes in grateful thanksgiving for what he had found, and he bent to kiss her.

* * * * *

Look for Jake McClennon's story in late 1995
from Silhouette Special Edition.

SILHOUETTE® *Desire*

M of the MAN Month 1995

Don't let the winter months get you down because the heat is about to get turned way up...with the sexiest hunks of 1995!

January: **A NUISANCE**
by **Lass Small**

February: **COWBOYS DON'T CRY**
by **Anne McAllister**

March: **THAT BURKE MAN**
the 75th Man of the Month
by **Diana Palmer**

April: **MR. EASY**
by **Cait London**

May: **MYSTERIOUS MOUNTAIN MAN**
by **Annette Broadrick**

June: **SINGLE DAD**
by **Jennifer Greene**

MAN OF THE MONTH...
ONLY FROM
SIILHOUETTE DESIRE

DREAM WEDDING
by Pamela Macaluso

Don't miss JUST MARRIED, a fun-filled series by Pamela Macaluso about three men with wealth, power and looks to die for. These bad boys had everything—except the love of a good woman.

***

"What a nerd!" Those taunting words played over and over in Alex Dalton's mind. Now that he was a rich, successful businessman—with looks to boot—he was going to make Genie Hill regret being so cruel to him in high school. All he had to do was seduce her…and then dump her. But could he do it without falling head over heels for her—again?

Find out in DREAM WEDDING, book two of the JUST MARRIED series, coming to you in May…only in

Take 4 bestselling love stories FREE

Plus get a FREE surprise gift!

Special Limited-time Offer

Mail to Silhouette Reader Service™

3010 Walden Avenue
P.O. Box 1867
Buffalo, N.Y. 14269-1867

YES! Please send me 4 free Silhouette Desire® novels and my free surprise gift. Then send me 6 brand-new novels every month, which I will receive months before they appear in bookstores. Bill me at the low price of $2.44 each plus 25¢ delivery and applicable sales tax, if any.* That's the complete price and a savings of over 10% off the cover prices—quite a bargain! I understand that accepting the books and gift places me under no obligation ever to buy any books. I can always return a shipment and cancel at any time. Even if I never buy another book from Silhouette, the 4 free books and the surprise gift are mine to keep forever.

225 BPA ANRS

Name	(PLEASE PRINT)	
Address	Apt. No.	
City	State	Zip

This offer is limited to one order per household and not valid to present Silhouette Desire® subscribers. *Terms and prices are subject to change without notice.
Sales tax applicable in N.Y.

UDES-295 ©1990 Harlequin Enterprises Limited

COMING NEXT MONTH

#931 SINGLE DAD—Jennifer Greene

June's *Man of the Month*, Josh Penoyer, had no time for women in his hectic life. But his kids wanted a new mom, and they'd decided beautiful Ariel Lindstrom would be perfect for the job!

#932 THE ENGAGEMENT PARTY—Barbara Boswell

Always a Bridesmaid!

When Hannah Farley attended her friend's engagement party, she never thought she could be the next one walking down the aisle, *especially* with an arrogant yet sexy stranger named Matthew Granger....

#933 DR. DADDY—Liz Bevarly

From Here to Maternity

Working with redhead Zoey Holland was more than Dr. Jonas Tate could stand. But when he needed advice for raising his niece, he found himself asking Zoey—and *wanting* the feisty woman....

#934 ANNIE SAYS I DO—Carole Buck

Wedding Belles

Annie Martin and Matt Powell had been inseparable friends since they were kids. Now a "pretend" date had Matt wondering how to get his independent and suddenly irresistible friend to say "I do!"

#935 HESITANT HUSBAND—Jackie Merritt

Mitch Conover refused to fall for his new boss's daughter, no matter what the sexy woman made him feel. But Kim Armstrong wouldn't give up until she worked her way into his heart....

#936 RANCHER'S WIFE—Anne Marie Winston

Angel Davis needed a vacation—not a headstrong rancher named Day Ryder to boss her around. But it wasn't long before she fell for his little girl...and the stubborn rancher *himself!*

Announcing
the New Pages & Privileges™ Program
from Harlequin® and Silhouette®

Get All This FREE
With Just One Proof-of-Purchase!

- **FREE Travel Service** with the guaranteed lowest available airfares plus 5% cash back on every ticket

- **FREE Hotel Discounts** of up to 60% off at leading hotels in the U.S., Canada and Europe

- **FREE Petite Parfumerie** collection (a $50 Retail value)

- **FREE $25 Travel Voucher** to use on any ticket on any airline booked through our Travel Service

- **FREE Insider Tips Letter** full of fascinating information and hot sneak previews of upcoming books

- **FREE Mystery Gift** (if you enroll before May 31/95)

And there are more great gifts and benefits to come!
Enroll today and become Privileged!

(see insert for details)

PROOF-OF-PURCHASE

Offer expires October 31, 1996   SD-PP1